THE ADVENTURES OF THE GRAND VIZIER IZNOGOUD
BY GOSCINNY & TABARY

THE WICKED WILES OF
IZNOGOUD

SCRIPT: GOSCINNY   **DRAWING: TABARY**

9th CINEBOOK
The 9th Art Publisher

COMING SOON

AUGUST 2008

Original title: Les complots d'Iznogoud

Original edition: © DARGAUD EDITEUR PARIS 1967 by Goscinny & Tabary
www.dargaud.com

Lettering and Text layout: Imadjinn sarl
Printed in Spain by Just Colour Graphic

This edition published in Great Britain in 2008 by
CINEBOOK Ltd
56 Beech Avenue
Canterbury, Kent
CT4 7TA
www.cinebook.com

A CIP catalogue record for this book is available from the British Library

ISBN 978-1-905460-46-5

9th CINEBOOK
The 9th Art Publisher

THERE WAS IN BAGHDAD THE MAGNIFICENT A GRAND VIZIER (5 FEET TALL IN HIS POINTY SLIPPERS) NAMED IZNOGOUD. HE WAS TRULY NASTY AND HAD ONLY ONE GOAL...

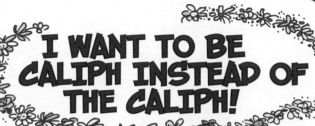

I WANT TO BE CALIPH INSTEAD OF THE CALIPH!

I WANT TO BE CALIPH INSTEAD OF THE CALIPH!

THIS VILE, NARROW-MINDED GRAND VIZIER HAD A FAITHFUL STRONG-ARM MAN NAMED WA'AT ALAHF. THIS FELLOW, DESPITE HIS NAME, DIDN'T LAUGH VERY OFTEN.

ALWAYS FOR PHOTOS.

I WANT TO BE CALIPH INSTEAD OF THE CALIPH!

WHILE THE CALIPH OF BAGHDAD, THE GOOD HAROUN AL PLASSID, WHO HAD ABSOLUTE CONFIDENCE IN HIS GRAND VIZIER, PASSED HIS HAPPY, SLEEPY DAYS IN THE SWEET SERENITY OF HIS SOVEREIGNTY.

I AM AT PEACE.

TABARY

NOW THEN, TO BAGHDAD THE MAGNIFICENT...

"KISSMET"

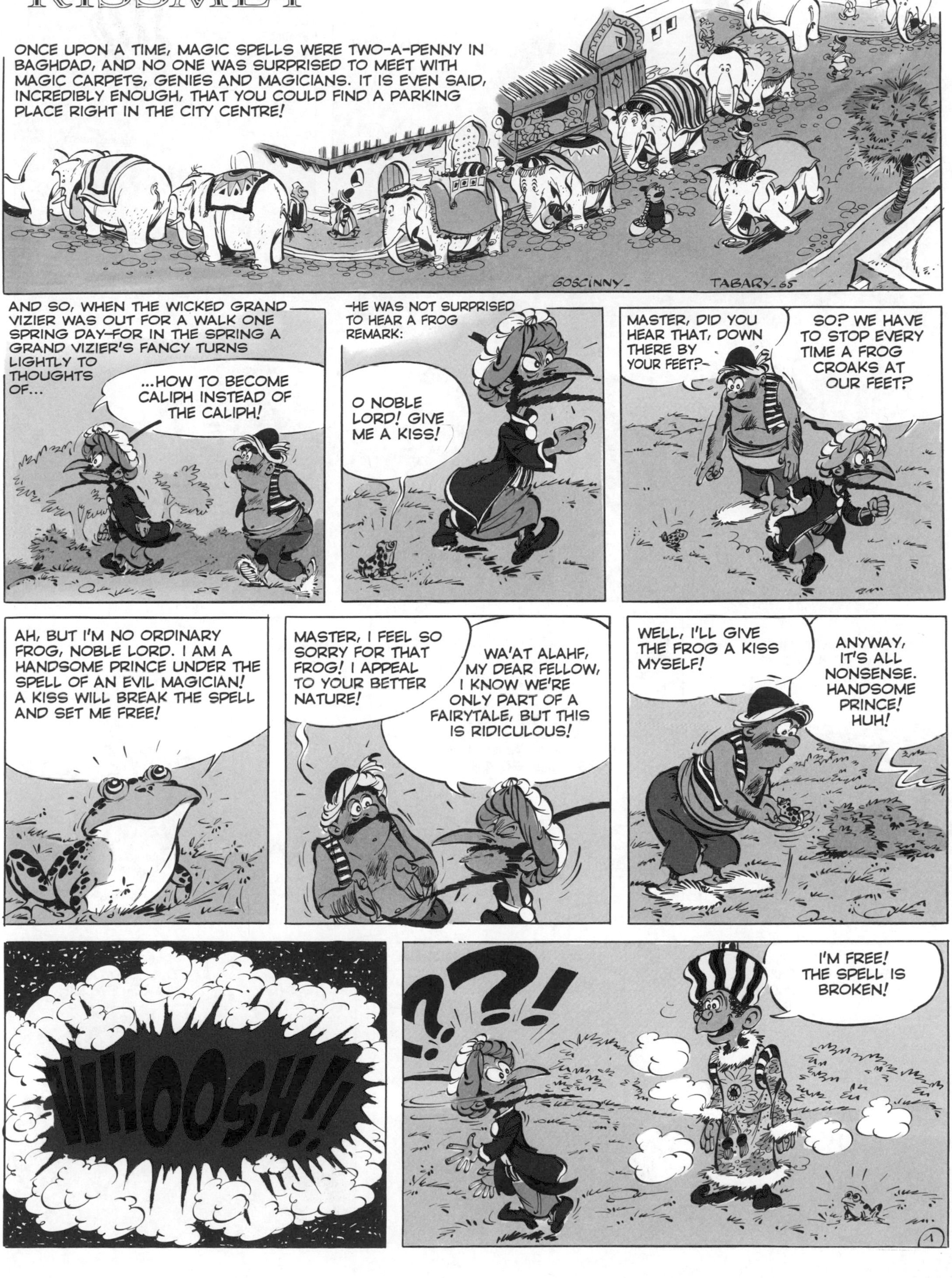
ONCE UPON A TIME, MAGIC SPELLS WERE TWO-A-PENNY IN BAGHDAD, AND NO ONE WAS SURPRISED TO MEET WITH MAGIC CARPETS, GENIES AND MAGICIANS. IT IS EVEN SAID, INCREDIBLY ENOUGH, THAT YOU COULD FIND A PARKING PLACE RIGHT IN THE CITY CENTRE!
GOSCINNY- TABARY-65
AND SO, WHEN THE WICKED GRAND VIZIER WAS OUT FOR A WALK ONE SPRING DAY–FOR IN THE SPRING A GRAND VIZIER'S FANCY TURNS LIGHTLY TO THOUGHTS OF...
...HOW TO BECOME CALIPH INSTEAD OF THE CALIPH!
–HE WAS NOT SURPRISED TO HEAR A FROG REMARK:
O NOBLE LORD! GIVE ME A KISS!
MASTER, DID YOU HEAR THAT, DOWN THERE BY YOUR FEET?–
SO? WE HAVE TO STOP EVERY TIME A FROG CROAKS AT OUR FEET?
AH, BUT I'M NO ORDINARY FROG, NOBLE LORD. I AM A HANDSOME PRINCE UNDER THE SPELL OF AN EVIL MAGICIAN! A KISS WILL BREAK THE SPELL AND SET ME FREE!
MASTER, I FEEL SO SORRY FOR THAT FROG! I APPEAL TO YOUR BETTER NATURE!
WA'AT ALAHF, MY DEAR FELLOW, I KNOW WE'RE ONLY PART OF A FAIRYTALE, BUT THIS IS RIDICULOUS!
WELL, I'LL GIVE THE FROG A KISS MYSELF!
ANYWAY, IT'S ALL NONSENSE. HANDSOME PRINCE! HUH!
WHOOSH!!
?!?!
I'M FREE! THE SPELL IS BROKEN!
1

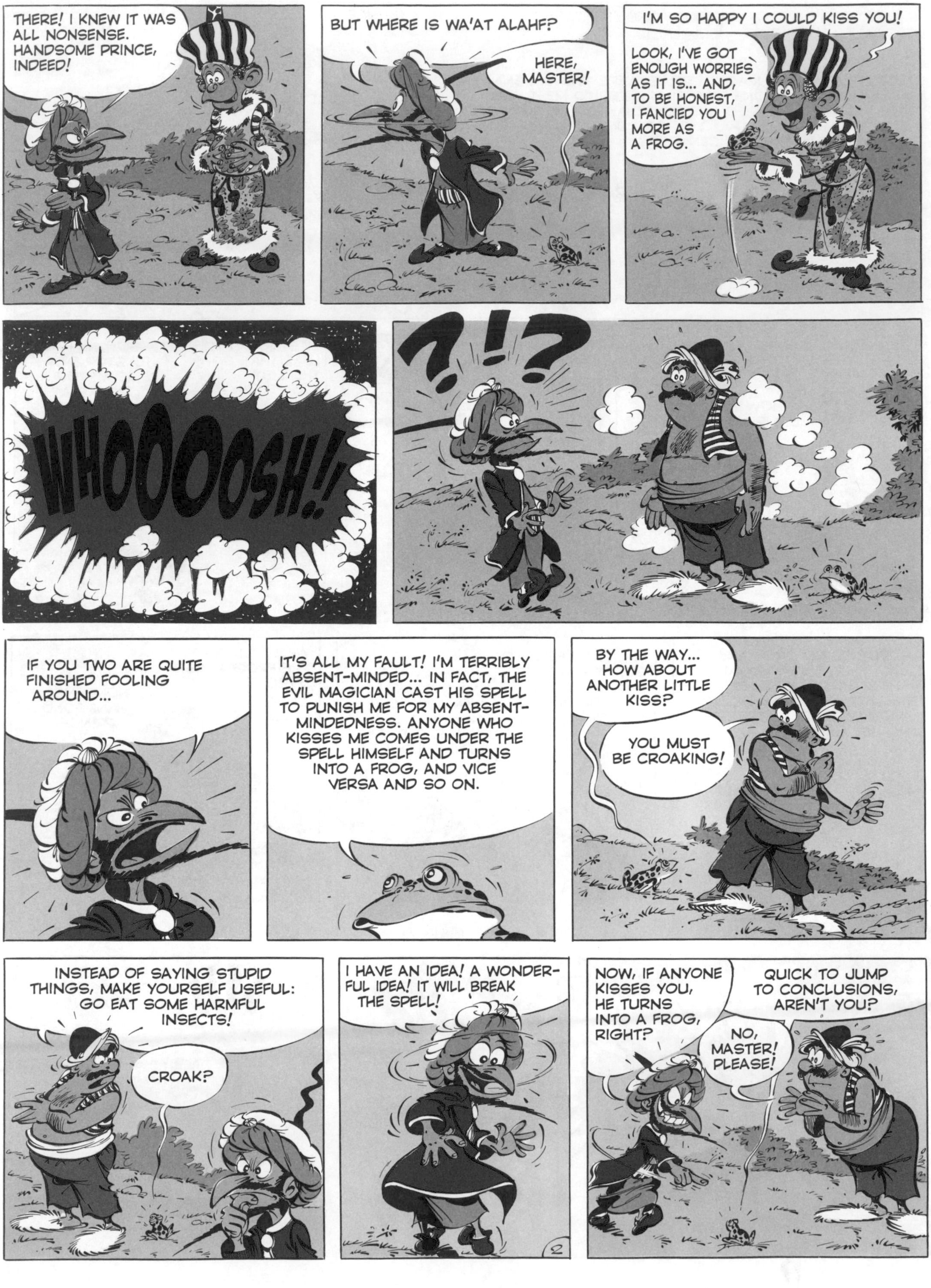

THERE! I KNEW IT WAS ALL NONSENSE. HANDSOME PRINCE, INDEED!
BUT WHERE IS WA'AT ALAHF?
HERE, MASTER!
I'M SO HAPPY I COULD KISS YOU!
LOOK, I'VE GOT ENOUGH WORRIES AS IT IS... AND, TO BE HONEST, I FANCIED YOU MORE AS A FROG.
WHOOOOOSH!!
?!?
IF YOU TWO ARE QUITE FINISHED FOOLING AROUND...
IT'S ALL MY FAULT! I'M TERRIBLY ABSENT-MINDED... IN FACT, THE EVIL MAGICIAN CAST HIS SPELL TO PUNISH ME FOR MY ABSENT-MINDEDNESS. ANYONE WHO KISSES ME COMES UNDER THE SPELL HIMSELF AND TURNS INTO A FROG, AND VICE VERSA AND SO ON.
BY THE WAY... HOW ABOUT ANOTHER LITTLE KISS?
YOU MUST BE CROAKING!
INSTEAD OF SAYING STUPID THINGS, MAKE YOURSELF USEFUL: GO EAT SOME HARMFUL INSECTS!
CROAK?
I HAVE AN IDEA! A WONDERFUL IDEA! IT WILL BREAK THE SPELL!
NOW, IF ANYONE KISSES YOU, HE TURNS INTO A FROG, RIGHT?
QUICK TO JUMP TO CONCLUSIONS, AREN'T YOU?
NO, MASTER! PLEASE!

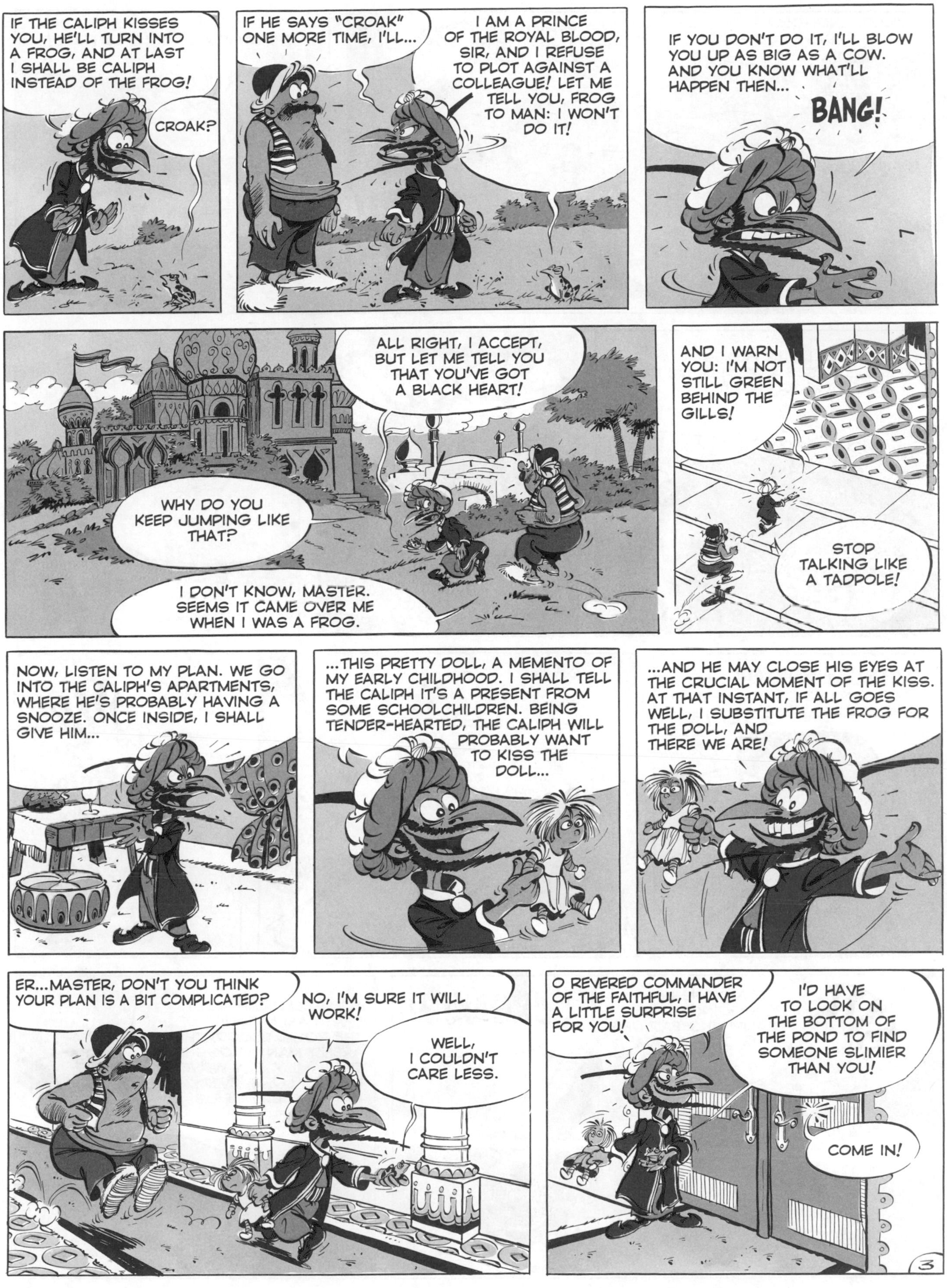

IF THE CALIPH KISSES YOU, HE'LL TURN INTO A FROG, AND AT LAST I SHALL BE CALIPH INSTEAD OF THE FROG!
CROAK?
IF HE SAYS "CROAK" ONE MORE TIME, I'LL...
I AM A PRINCE OF THE ROYAL BLOOD, SIR, AND I REFUSE TO PLOT AGAINST A COLLEAGUE! LET ME TELL YOU, FROG TO MAN: I WON'T DO IT!
IF YOU DON'T DO IT, I'LL BLOW YOU UP AS BIG AS A COW. AND YOU KNOW WHAT'LL HAPPEN THEN...
BANG!
ALL RIGHT, I ACCEPT, BUT LET ME TELL YOU THAT YOU'VE GOT A BLACK HEART!
WHY DO YOU KEEP JUMPING LIKE THAT?
I DON'T KNOW, MASTER. SEEMS IT CAME OVER ME WHEN I WAS A FROG.
AND I WARN YOU: I'M NOT STILL GREEN BEHIND THE GILLS!
STOP TALKING LIKE A TADPOLE!
NOW, LISTEN TO MY PLAN. WE GO INTO THE CALIPH'S APARTMENTS, WHERE HE'S PROBABLY HAVING A SNOOZE. ONCE INSIDE, I SHALL GIVE HIM...
...THIS PRETTY DOLL, A MEMENTO OF MY EARLY CHILDHOOD. I SHALL TELL THE CALIPH IT'S A PRESENT FROM SOME SCHOOLCHILDREN. BEING TENDER-HEARTED, THE CALIPH WILL PROBABLY WANT TO KISS THE DOLL...
...AND HE MAY CLOSE HIS EYES AT THE CRUCIAL MOMENT OF THE KISS. AT THAT INSTANT, IF ALL GOES WELL, I SUBSTITUTE THE FROG FOR THE DOLL, AND THERE WE ARE!
ER...MASTER, DON'T YOU THINK YOUR PLAN IS A BIT COMPLICATED?
NO, I'M SURE IT WILL WORK!
WELL, I COULDN'T CARE LESS.
O REVERED COMMANDER OF THE FAITHFUL, I HAVE A LITTLE SURPRISE FOR YOU!
I'D HAVE TO LOOK ON THE BOTTOM OF THE POND TO FIND SOMEONE SLIMIER THAN YOU!
COME IN!
3

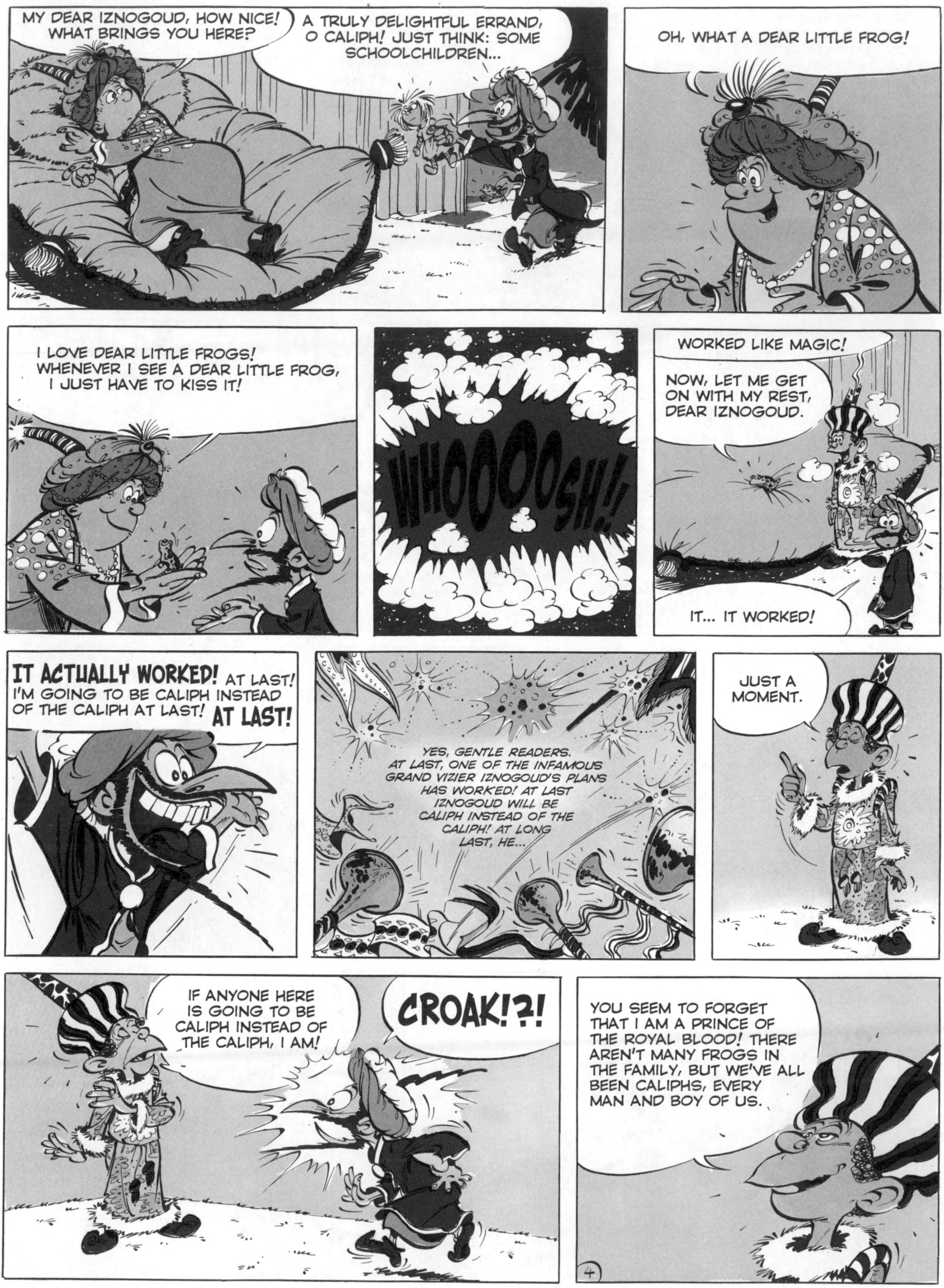
MY DEAR IZNOGOUD, HOW NICE! WHAT BRINGS YOU HERE?
A TRULY DELIGHTFUL ERRAND, O CALIPH! JUST THINK: SOME SCHOOLCHILDREN...
OH, WHAT A DEAR LITTLE FROG!
I LOVE DEAR LITTLE FROGS! WHENEVER I SEE A DEAR LITTLE FROG, I JUST HAVE TO KISS IT!
WHOOOOOSH!!
WORKED LIKE MAGIC!
NOW, LET ME GET ON WITH MY REST, DEAR IZNOGOUD.
IT... IT WORKED!
IT ACTUALLY WORKED! AT LAST! I'M GOING TO BE CALIPH INSTEAD OF THE CALIPH AT LAST! AT LAST!
YES, GENTLE READERS. AT LAST, ONE OF THE INFAMOUS GRAND VIZIER IZNOGOUD'S PLANS HAS WORKED! AT LAST IZNOGOUD WILL BE CALIPH INSTEAD OF THE CALIPH! AT LONG LAST, HE...
JUST A MOMENT.
IF ANYONE HERE IS GOING TO BE CALIPH INSTEAD OF THE CALIPH, I AM!
CROAK!?!
YOU SEEM TO FORGET THAT I AM A PRINCE OF THE ROYAL BLOOD! THERE AREN'T MANY FROGS IN THE FAMILY, BUT WE'VE ALL BEEN CALIPHS, EVERY MAN AND BOY OF US.
4

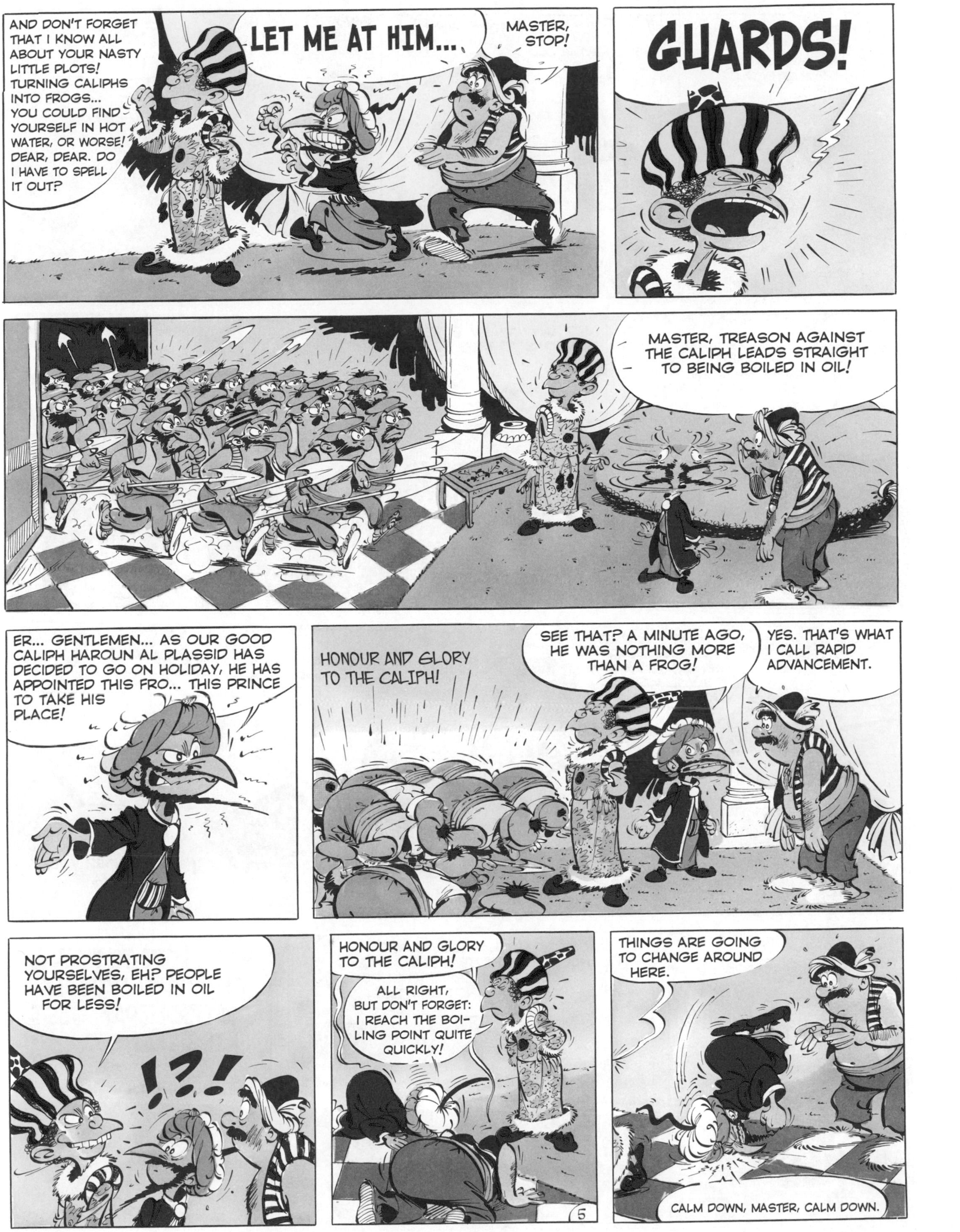
AND DON'T FORGET THAT I KNOW ALL ABOUT YOUR NASTY LITTLE PLOTS! TURNING CALIPHS INTO FROGS... YOU COULD FIND YOURSELF IN HOT WATER, OR WORSE! DEAR, DEAR. DO I HAVE TO SPELL IT OUT?
LET ME AT HIM...
MASTER, STOP!
GUARDS!
MASTER, TREASON AGAINST THE CALIPH LEADS STRAIGHT TO BEING BOILED IN OIL!
ER... GENTLEMEN... AS OUR GOOD CALIPH HAROUN AL PLASSID HAS DECIDED TO GO ON HOLIDAY, HE HAS APPOINTED THIS FRO... THIS PRINCE TO TAKE HIS PLACE!
HONOUR AND GLORY TO THE CALIPH!
SEE THAT? A MINUTE AGO, HE WAS NOTHING MORE THAN A FROG!
YES. THAT'S WHAT I CALL RAPID ADVANCEMENT.
NOT PROSTRATING YOURSELVES, EH? PEOPLE HAVE BEEN BOILED IN OIL FOR LESS!
!?!
HONOUR AND GLORY TO THE CALIPH!
ALL RIGHT, BUT DON'T FORGET: I REACH THE BOILING POINT QUITE QUICKLY!
5
THINGS ARE GOING TO CHANGE AROUND HERE.
CALM DOWN, MASTER, CALM DOWN.

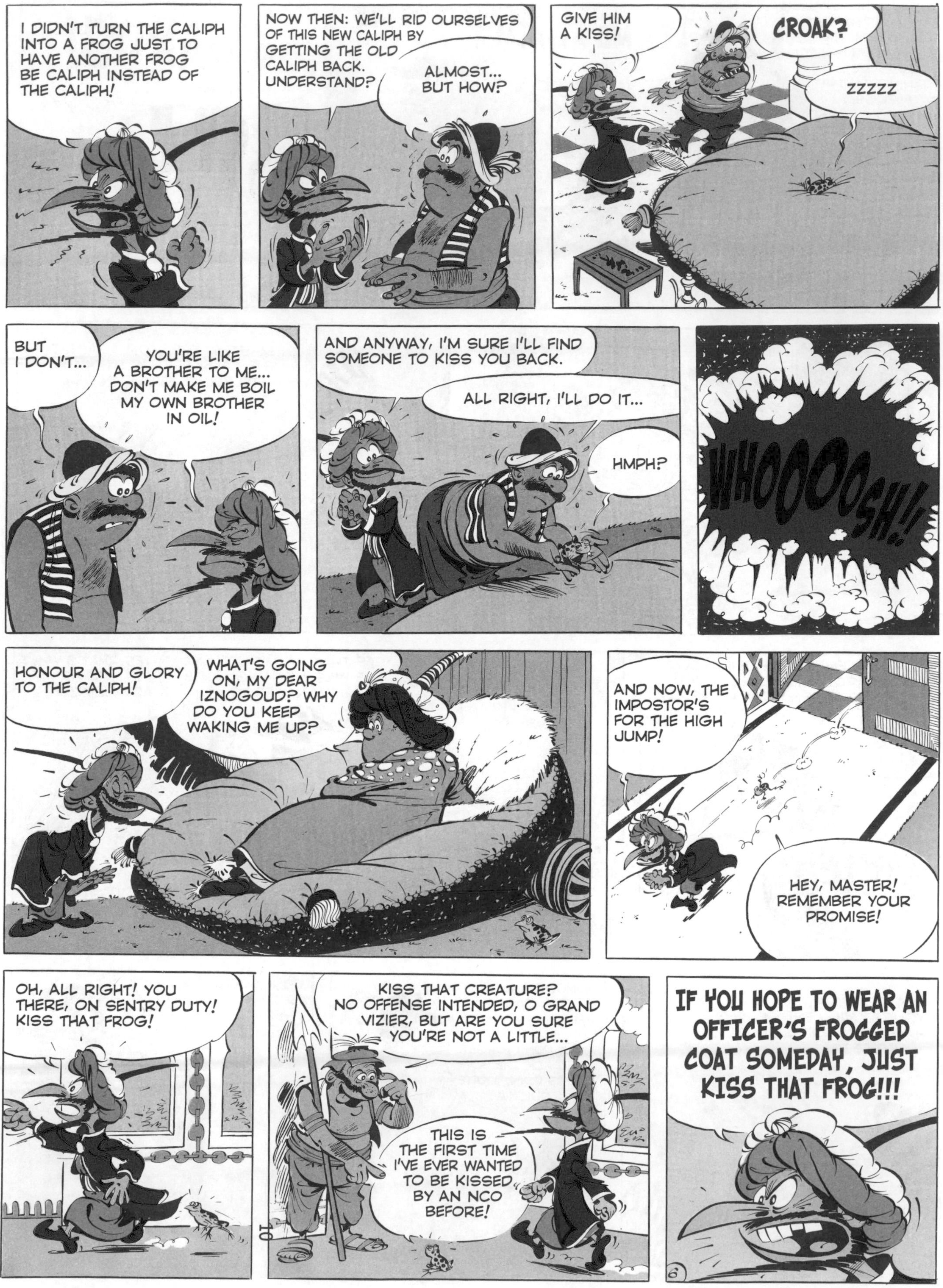
I DIDN'T TURN THE CALIPH INTO A FROG JUST TO HAVE ANOTHER FROG BE CALIPH INSTEAD OF THE CALIPH!
NOW THEN: WE'LL RID OURSELVES OF THIS NEW CALIPH BY GETTING THE OLD CALIPH BACK. UNDERSTAND?
ALMOST... BUT HOW?
GIVE HIM A KISS!
CROAK?
ZZZZZ
BUT I DON'T...
YOU'RE LIKE A BROTHER TO ME... DON'T MAKE ME BOIL MY OWN BROTHER IN OIL!
AND ANYWAY, I'M SURE I'LL FIND SOMEONE TO KISS YOU BACK.
ALL RIGHT, I'LL DO IT...
HMPH?
WHOOOOOSH!!
HONOUR AND GLORY TO THE CALIPH!
WHAT'S GOING ON, MY DEAR IZNOGOUD? WHY DO YOU KEEP WAKING ME UP?
AND NOW, THE IMPOSTOR'S FOR THE HIGH JUMP!
HEY, MASTER! REMEMBER YOUR PROMISE!
OH, ALL RIGHT! YOU THERE, ON SENTRY DUTY! KISS THAT FROG!
KISS THAT CREATURE? NO OFFENSE INTENDED, O GRAND VIZIER, BUT ARE YOU SURE YOU'RE NOT A LITTLE...
THIS IS THE FIRST TIME I'VE EVER WANTED TO BE KISSED BY AN NCO BEFORE!
IF YOU HOPE TO WEAR AN OFFICER'S FROGGED COAT SOMEDAY, JUST KISS THAT FROG!!!

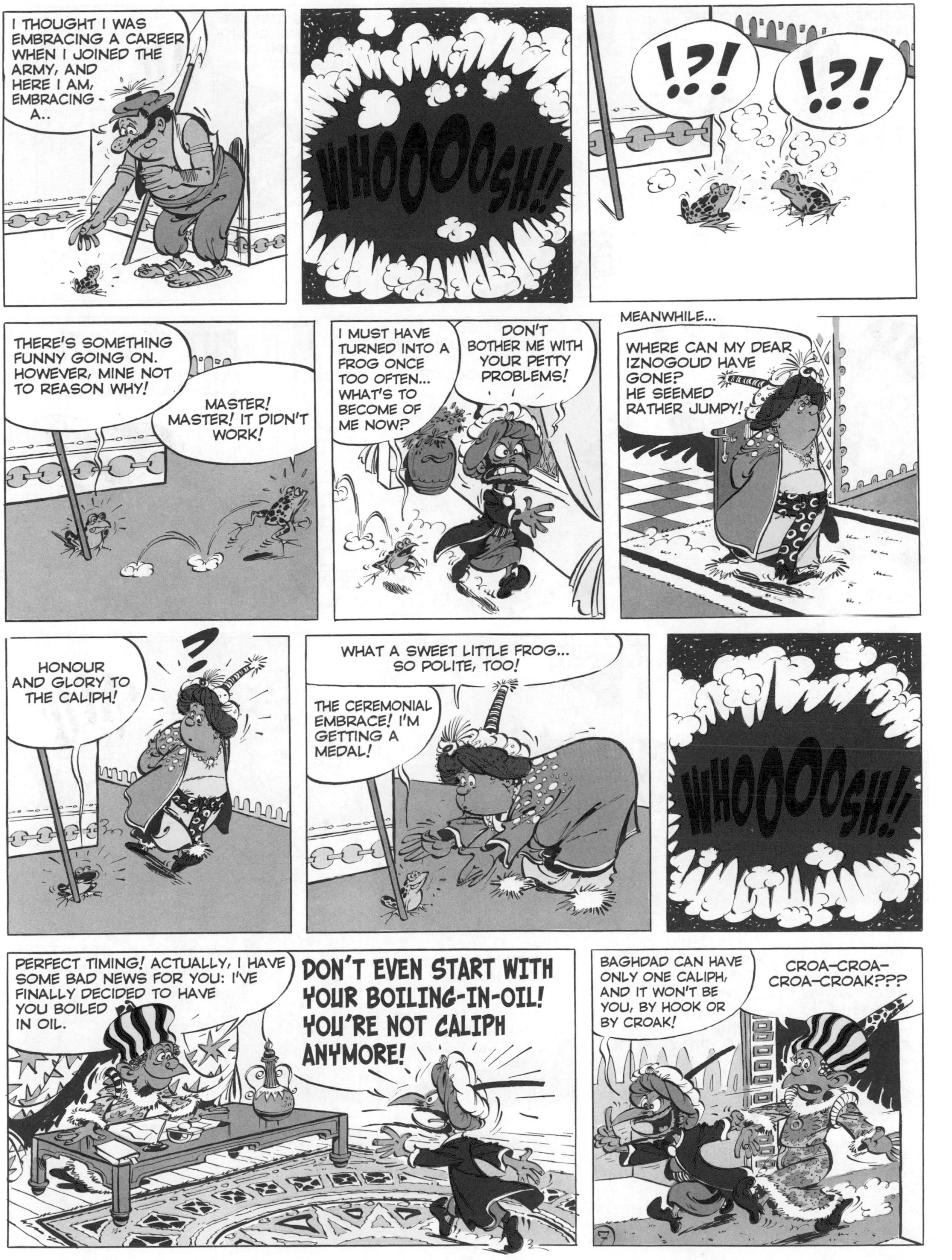
I THOUGHT I WAS EMBRACING A CAREER WHEN I JOINED THE ARMY, AND HERE I AM, EMBRACING - A..
WHOOOOOSH!!
!?!
!?!
THERE'S SOMETHING FUNNY GOING ON. HOWEVER, MINE NOT TO REASON WHY!
MASTER! MASTER! IT DIDN'T WORK!
I MUST HAVE TURNED INTO A FROG ONCE TOO OFTEN... WHAT'S TO BECOME OF ME NOW?
DON'T BOTHER ME WITH YOUR PETTY PROBLEMS!
MEANWHILE...
WHERE CAN MY DEAR IZNOGOUD HAVE GONE? HE SEEMED RATHER JUMPY!
HONOUR AND GLORY TO THE CALIPH!
WHAT A SWEET LITTLE FROG... SO POLITE, TOO!
THE CEREMONIAL EMBRACE! I'M GETTING A MEDAL!
WHOOOOOSH!!
PERFECT TIMING! ACTUALLY, I HAVE SOME BAD NEWS FOR YOU: I'VE FINALLY DECIDED TO HAVE YOU BOILED IN OIL.
DON'T EVEN START WITH YOUR BOILING-IN-OIL! YOU'RE NOT CALIPH ANYMORE!
BAGHDAD CAN HAVE ONLY ONE CALIPH, AND IT WON'T BE YOU, BY HOOK OR BY CROAK!
CROA-CROA-CROA-CROAK???

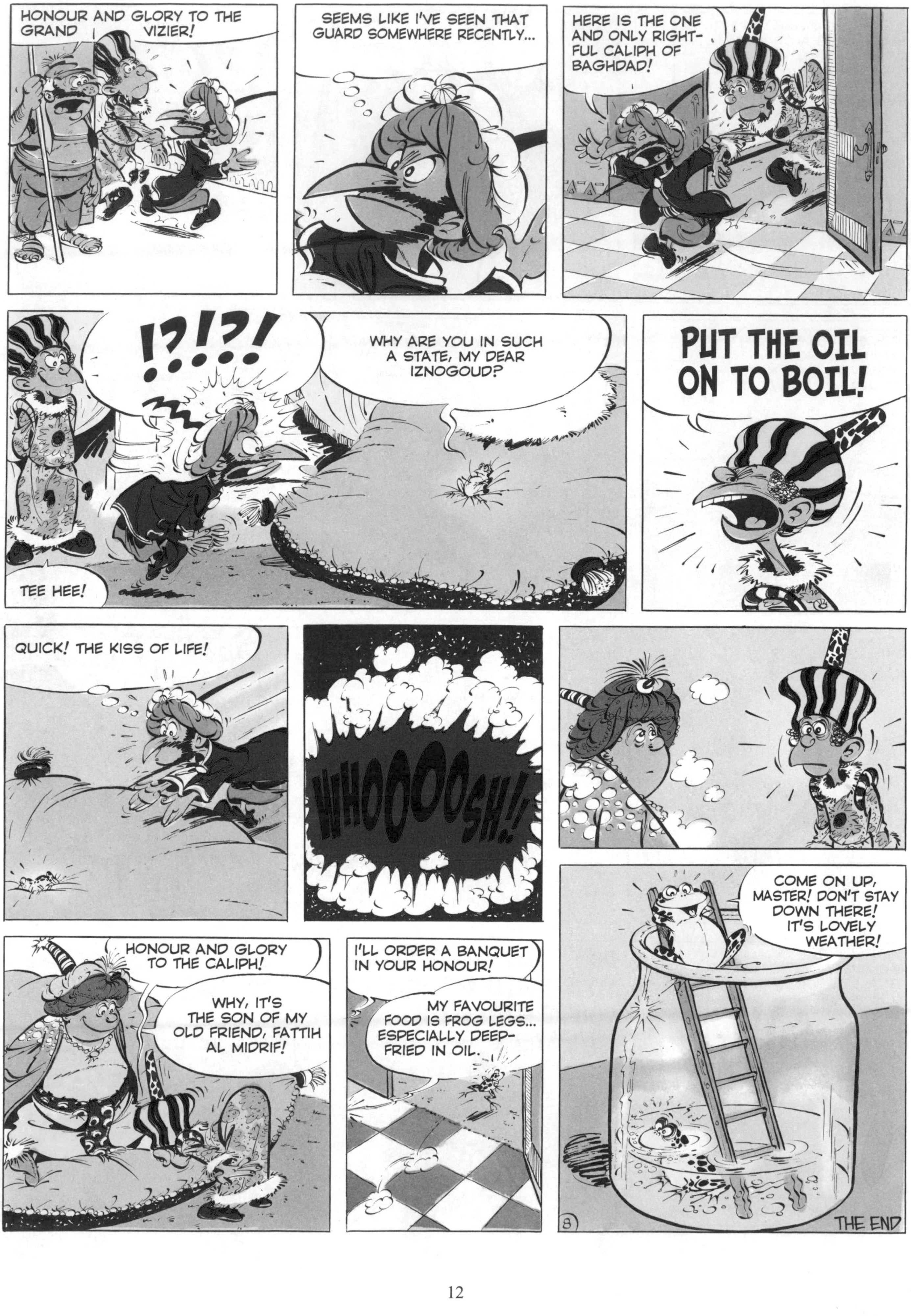

HONOUR AND GLORY TO THE GRAND VIZIER!
SEEMS LIKE I'VE SEEN THAT GUARD SOMEWHERE RECENTLY...
HERE IS THE ONE AND ONLY RIGHTFUL CALIPH OF BAGHDAD!
!?!?!
WHY ARE YOU IN SUCH A STATE, MY DEAR IZNOGOUD?
TEE HEE!
PUT THE OIL ON TO BOIL!
QUICK! THE KISS OF LIFE!
WHOOOOOSH!!
HONOUR AND GLORY TO THE CALIPH!
WHY, IT'S THE SON OF MY OLD FRIEND, FATTIH AL MIDRIF!
I'LL ORDER A BANQUET IN YOUR HONOUR!
MY FAVOURITE FOOD IS FROG LEGS... ESPECIALLY DEEP-FRIED IN OIL.
COME ON UP, MASTER! DON'T STAY DOWN THERE! IT'S LOVELY WEATHER!
8
THE END

MESMER-EYEZED

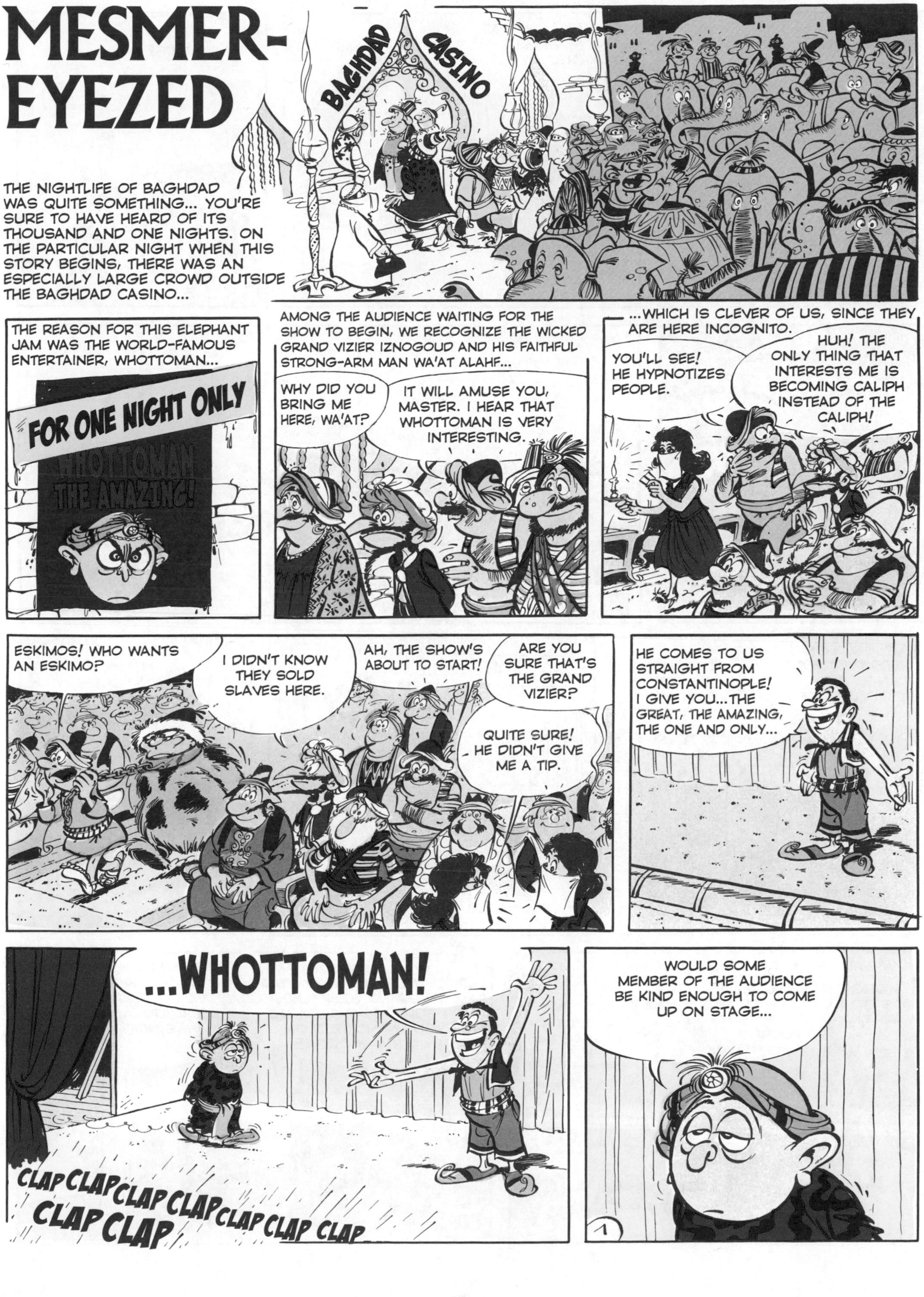

THE NIGHTLIFE OF BAGHDAD WAS QUITE SOMETHING... YOU'RE SURE TO HAVE HEARD OF ITS THOUSAND AND ONE NIGHTS. ON THE PARTICULAR NIGHT WHEN THIS STORY BEGINS, THERE WAS AN ESPECIALLY LARGE CROWD OUTSIDE THE BAGHDAD CASINO...
BAGHDAD CASINO
THE REASON FOR THIS ELEPHANT JAM WAS THE WORLD-FAMOUS ENTERTAINER, WHOTTOMAN...
FOR ONE NIGHT ONLY
WHOTTOMAN THE AMAZING!
AMONG THE AUDIENCE WAITING FOR THE SHOW TO BEGIN, WE RECOGNIZE THE WICKED GRAND VIZIER IZNOGOUD AND HIS FAITHFUL STRONG-ARM MAN WA'AT ALAHF...
WHY DID YOU BRING ME HERE, WA'AT?
IT WILL AMUSE YOU, MASTER. I HEAR THAT WHOTTOMAN IS VERY INTERESTING.
...WHICH IS CLEVER OF US, SINCE THEY ARE HERE INCOGNITO.
YOU'LL SEE! HE HYPNOTIZES PEOPLE.
HUH! THE ONLY THING THAT INTERESTS ME IS BECOMING CALIPH INSTEAD OF THE CALIPH!
ESKIMOS! WHO WANTS AN ESKIMO?
I DIDN'T KNOW THEY SOLD SLAVES HERE.
AH, THE SHOW'S ABOUT TO START!
ARE YOU SURE THAT'S THE GRAND VIZIER?
QUITE SURE! HE DIDN'T GIVE ME A TIP.
HE COMES TO US STRAIGHT FROM CONSTANTINOPLE! I GIVE YOU...THE GREAT, THE AMAZING, THE ONE AND ONLY...
...WHOTTOMAN!
CLAP CLAP CLAP CLAP CLAP CLAP CLAP CLAP CLAP CLAP
WOULD SOME MEMBER OF THE AUDIENCE BE KIND ENOUGH TO COME UP ON STAGE...
1

I WILL!

VERY WELL, YOUNG MAN! NOW, PLEASE LOOK INTO MY EYES!

LIKE THIS?

LIKE THAT!

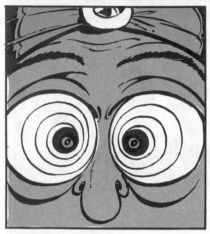

YOU ARE A CAT.

MEOW.

THERE!

WAIT A MOMENT! I NEED PURRFECT SILENCE! NO APPLAUSE, PLEASE!

PURRRRRR PURRRRR PURRRRR

GET OUT, YOU NASTY CREATURE!

MEEOOOW!

PAF

I CAN'T STAND CATS!

NOW, WILL SOME OTHER GENTLEMAN COME UP ON STAGE?

AMAZING! MARVELLOUS! LET'S GO AND WAIT FOR THIS WHOTTOMAN IN HIS DRESSING ROOM!

BUT WHAT ABOUT THE REST OF THE SHOW?

LATER...

WHOTTOMAN, I LIKED YOUR ACT VERY MUCH, I AM THE GRAND VIZIER IZNOGOUD, AND I SUPPOSE THE YOUNG MAN YOU HYPNOTIZED ON STAGE WAS A STOOGE?

THANK YOU FOR YOUR KIND WORDS, GRAND VIZIER, PLEASED TO MEET YOU, AND NO, HE WAS NOT A STOOGE.

2

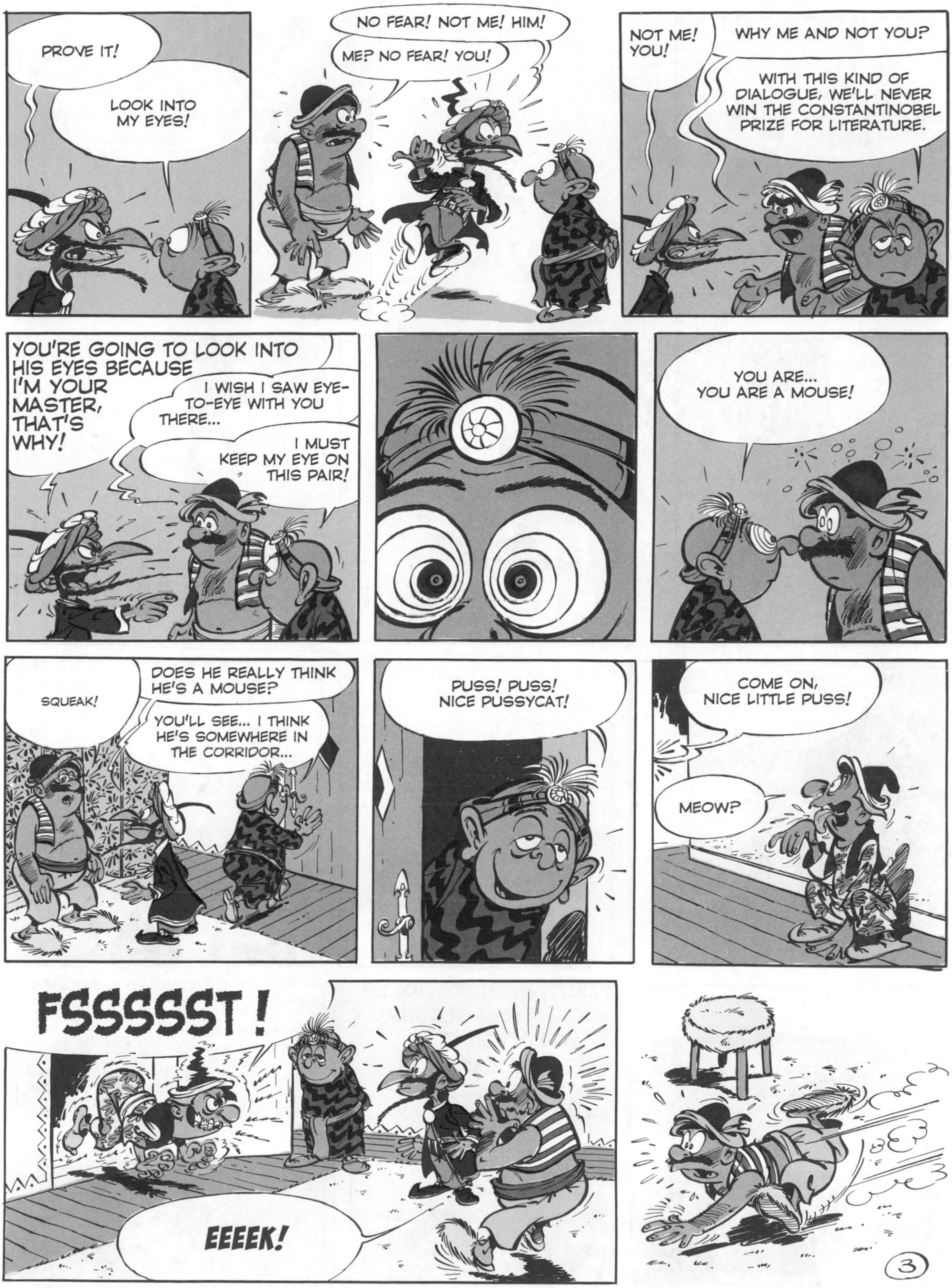
PROVE IT!
LOOK INTO MY EYES!
NO FEAR! NOT ME! HIM!
ME? NO FEAR! YOU!
NOT ME! YOU!
WHY ME AND NOT YOU?
WITH THIS KIND OF DIALOGUE, WE'LL NEVER WIN THE CONSTANTINOBEL PRIZE FOR LITERATURE.
YOU'RE GOING TO LOOK INTO HIS EYES BECAUSE I'M YOUR MASTER, THAT'S WHY!
I WISH I SAW EYE-TO-EYE WITH YOU THERE...
I MUST KEEP MY EYE ON THIS PAIR!
YOU ARE... YOU ARE A MOUSE!
SQUEAK!
DOES HE REALLY THINK HE'S A MOUSE?
YOU'LL SEE... I THINK HE'S SOMEWHERE IN THE CORRIDOR...
PUSS! PUSS! NICE PUSSYCAT!
COME ON, NICE LITTLE PUSS!
MEOW?
FSSSSST !
EEEEK!
3

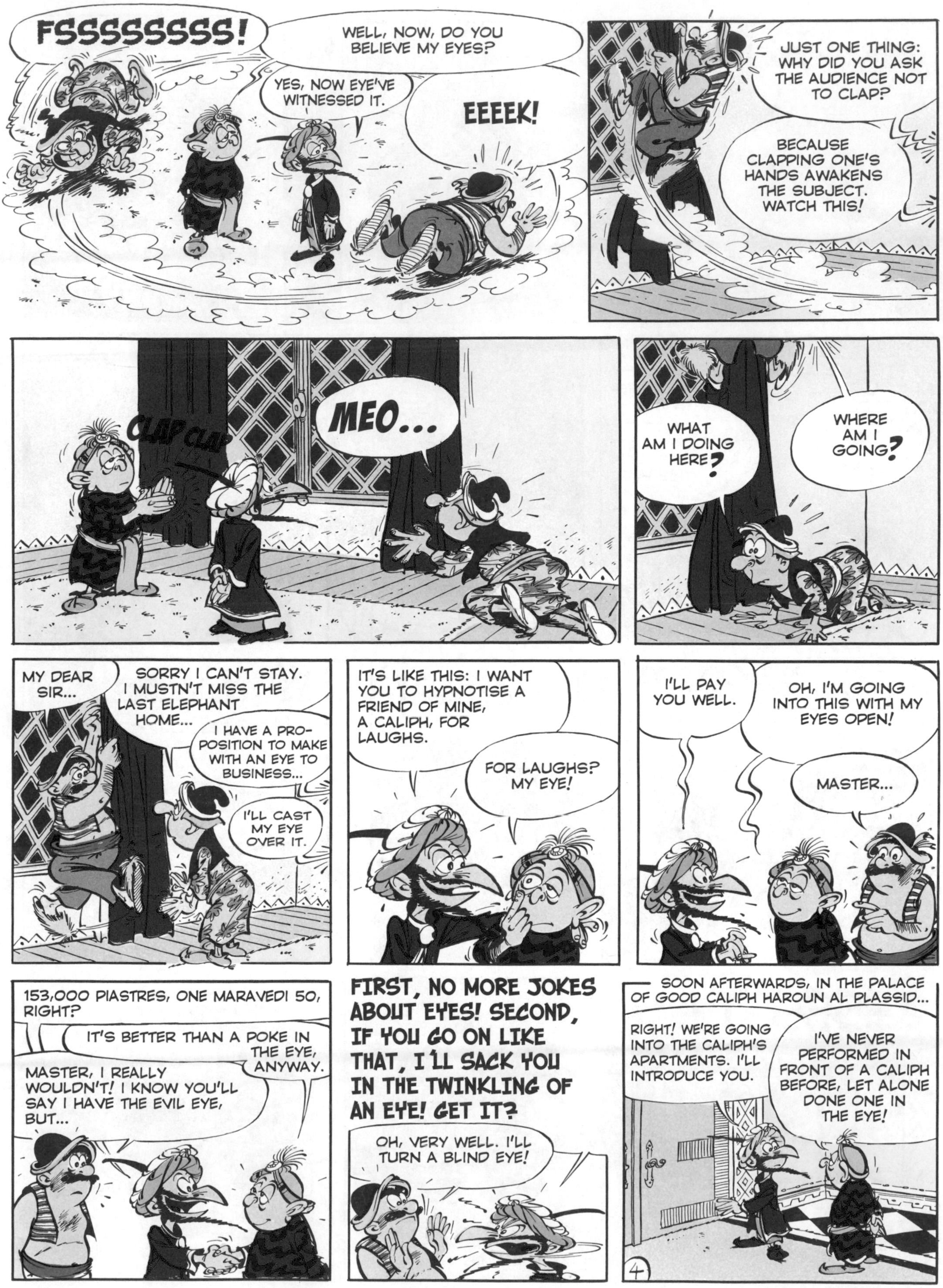
FSSSSSSSS!
WELL, NOW, DO YOU BELIEVE MY EYES?
YES, NOW EYE'VE WITNESSED IT.
EEEEK!
JUST ONE THING: WHY DID YOU ASK THE AUDIENCE NOT TO CLAP?
BECAUSE CLAPPING ONE'S HANDS AWAKENS THE SUBJECT. WATCH THIS!
CLAP CLAP
MEO...
WHAT AM I DOING HERE?
WHERE AM I GOING?
MY DEAR SIR...
SORRY I CAN'T STAY. I MUSTN'T MISS THE LAST ELEPHANT HOME...
I HAVE A PROPOSITION TO MAKE WITH AN EYE TO BUSINESS...
I'LL CAST MY EYE OVER IT.
IT'S LIKE THIS: I WANT YOU TO HYPNOTISE A FRIEND OF MINE, A CALIPH, FOR LAUGHS.
FOR LAUGHS? MY EYE!
I'LL PAY YOU WELL.
OH, I'M GOING INTO THIS WITH MY EYES OPEN!
MASTER...
153,000 PIASTRES, ONE MARAVEDI 50, RIGHT?
IT'S BETTER THAN A POKE IN THE EYE, ANYWAY.
MASTER, I REALLY WOULDN'T! I KNOW YOU'LL SAY I HAVE THE EVIL EYE, BUT...
FIRST, NO MORE JOKES ABOUT EYES! SECOND, IF YOU GO ON LIKE THAT, I'LL SACK YOU IN THE TWINKLING OF AN EYE! GET IT?
OH, VERY WELL. I'LL TURN A BLIND EYE!
SOON AFTERWARDS, IN THE PALACE OF GOOD CALIPH HAROUN AL PLASSID...
RIGHT! WE'RE GOING INTO THE CALIPH'S APARTMENTS. I'LL INTRODUCE YOU.
I'VE NEVER PERFORMED IN FRONT OF A CALIPH BEFORE, LET ALONE DONE ONE IN THE EYE!
4

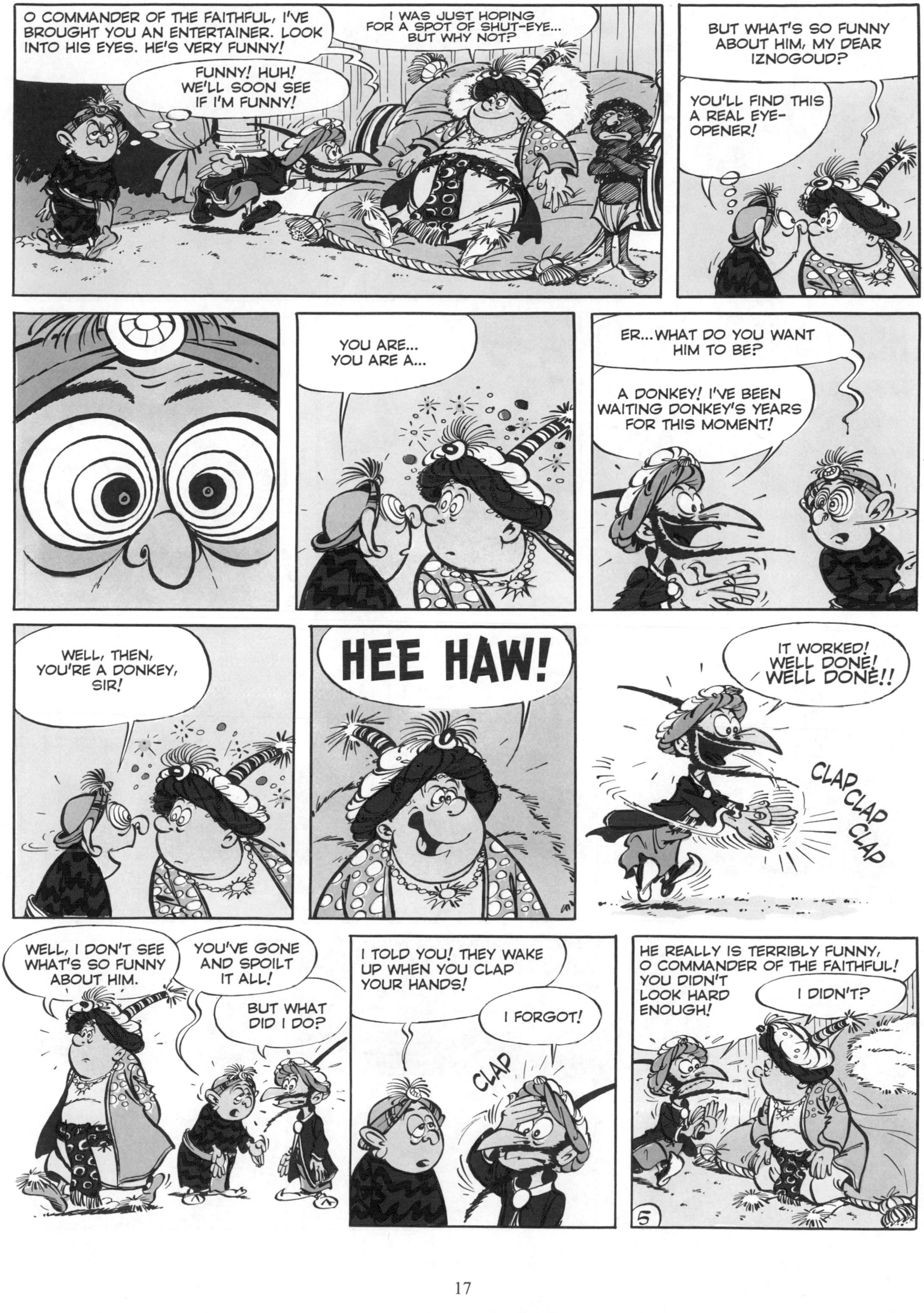
O COMMANDER OF THE FAITHFUL, I'VE BROUGHT YOU AN ENTERTAINER. LOOK INTO HIS EYES. HE'S VERY FUNNY!
FUNNY! HUH! WE'LL SOON SEE IF I'M FUNNY!
I WAS JUST HOPING FOR A SPOT OF SHUT-EYE... BUT WHY NOT?
BUT WHAT'S SO FUNNY ABOUT HIM, MY DEAR IZNOGOUD?
YOU'LL FIND THIS A REAL EYE-OPENER!
YOU ARE... YOU ARE A...
ER...WHAT DO YOU WANT HIM TO BE?
A DONKEY! I'VE BEEN WAITING DONKEY'S YEARS FOR THIS MOMENT!
WELL, THEN, YOU'RE A DONKEY, SIR!
HEE HAW!
IT WORKED! WELL DONE! WELL DONE!!
CLAP CLAP CLAP
WELL, I DON'T SEE WHAT'S SO FUNNY ABOUT HIM.
YOU'VE GONE AND SPOILT IT ALL!
BUT WHAT DID I DO?
I TOLD YOU! THEY WAKE UP WHEN YOU CLAP YOUR HANDS!
I FORGOT!
CLAP
HE REALLY IS TERRIBLY FUNNY, O COMMANDER OF THE FAITHFUL! YOU DIDN'T LOOK HARD ENOUGH!
I DIDN'T?
5

WELL, LET'S SEE WHAT'S SO FUNNY.

LOOK INTO MY EYES... YOU'LL SOON SEE IF IT'S EYEWASH!

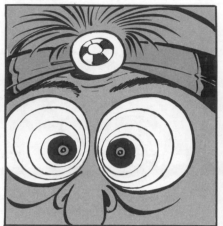

YOU ARE A DONKEY!

HEE HAW!

IT WORKED! IT WORKED!

?!?

CLAP CLAP

I'M SORRY. HE ISN'T VERY FUNNY.

WHO WENT AND CLAPPED HIS HANDS?

ME!

WHO ARE YOU?

A MOSQUITEER.

ONE OF THE CALIPH'S CRACK TEAM OF MOSQUITEERS. THERE ARE THREE OR FOUR OF US ON DUTY IN THE PALACE. WHEN WE SEE A MOSQUITO... CLAP!

CLAP

NEVER A MOMENT'S PEACE. COME ON, YOU TWO. I KNOW WHERE WE CAN HAVE FUN!

BUT I DON'T WANT ANY MORE FUN, MY DEAR IZNOGOUD! I WANT A NICE SNOOZE!

RIGHT! WE'LL BE NICE AND QUIET HERE BESIDE THE POOL IN THE PALACE PARK.

LOOK INTO...

I KNOW, I KNOW, YOU'RE GOING TO BE FUNNY. DO HURRY UP. I DON'T WANT TO MISS MY NAP.

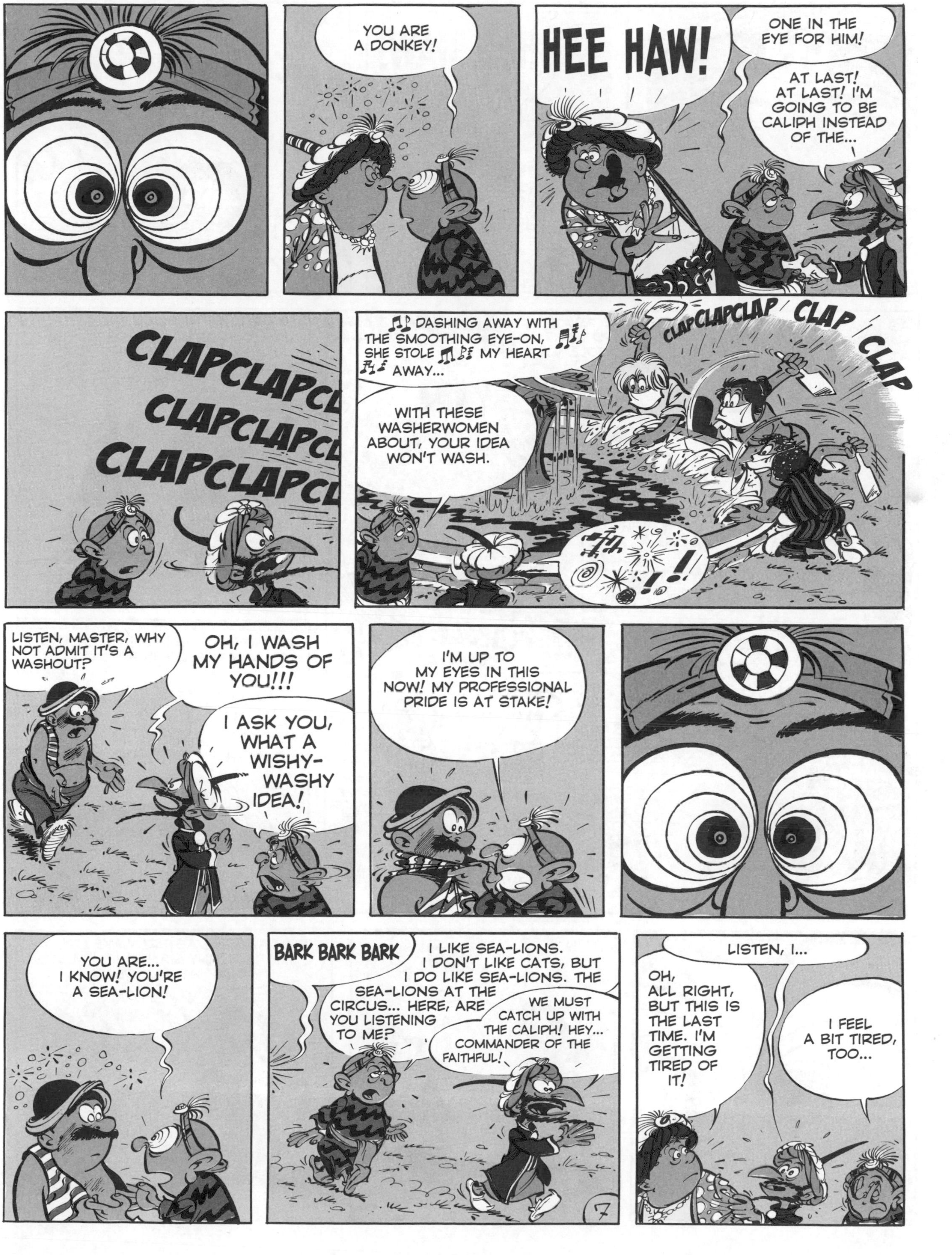
YOU ARE A DONKEY!
HEE HAW!
ONE IN THE EYE FOR HIM!
AT LAST! AT LAST! I'M GOING TO BE CALIPH INSTEAD OF THE...
CLAPCLAPCL
CLAPCLAPCL
CLAPCLAPCL
DASHING AWAY WITH THE SMOOTHING EYE-ON, SHE STOLE MY HEART AWAY...
CLAPCLAPCLAP CLAP CLAP
WITH THESE WASHERWOMEN ABOUT, YOUR IDEA WON'T WASH.
LISTEN, MASTER, WHY NOT ADMIT IT'S A WASHOUT?
OH, I WASH MY HANDS OF YOU!!!
I ASK YOU, WHAT A WISHY-WASHY IDEA!
I'M UP TO MY EYES IN THIS NOW! MY PROFESSIONAL PRIDE IS AT STAKE!
YOU ARE... I KNOW! YOU'RE A SEA-LION!
BARK BARK BARK
I LIKE SEA-LIONS. I DON'T LIKE CATS, BUT I DO LIKE SEA-LIONS. THE SEA-LIONS AT THE CIRCUS... HERE, ARE YOU LISTENING TO ME?
WE MUST CATCH UP WITH THE CALIPH! HEY... COMMANDER OF THE FAITHFUL!
LISTEN, I...
OH, ALL RIGHT, BUT THIS IS THE LAST TIME. I'M GETTING TIRED OF IT!
I FEEL A BIT TIRED, TOO...

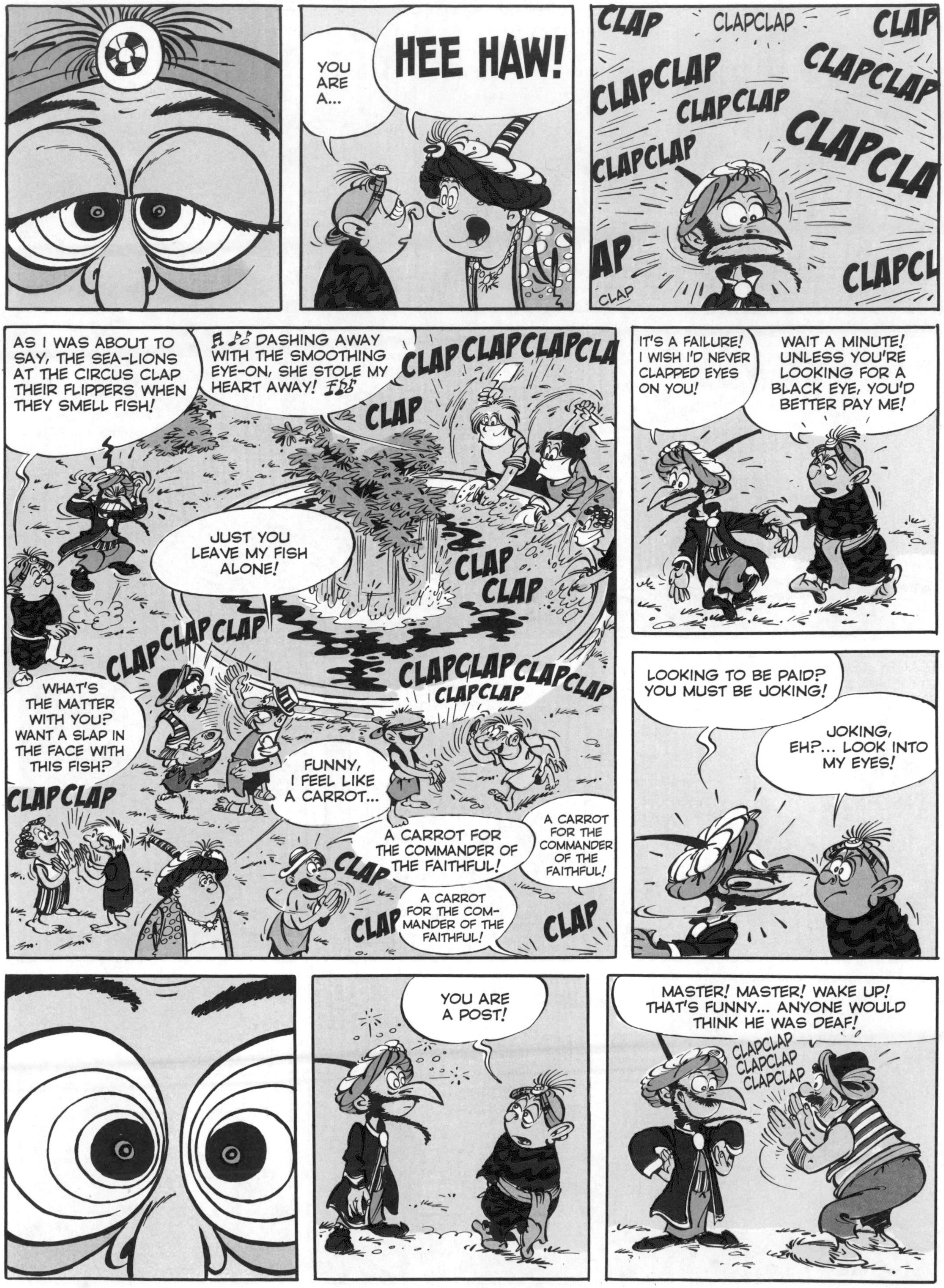
YOU ARE A...
HEE HAW!
CLAP CLAPCLAP CLAP CLAPCLAP CLAPCLAP CLAPCLAP CLAPCLAP CLAPCLA AP CLAPCL CLAP
AS I WAS ABOUT TO SAY, THE SEA-LIONS AT THE CIRCUS CLAP THEIR FLIPPERS WHEN THEY SMELL FISH!
DASHING AWAY WITH THE SMOOTHING EYE-ON, SHE STOLE MY HEART AWAY!
CLAPCLAPCLAPCLAPCLA
CLAP
JUST YOU LEAVE MY FISH ALONE!
CLAP CLAP
CLAPCLAPCLAP
CLAPCLAPCLAPCLAP CLAPCLAP
WHAT'S THE MATTER WITH YOU? WANT A SLAP IN THE FACE WITH THIS FISH?
CLAPCLAP
FUNNY, I FEEL LIKE A CARROT...
A CARROT FOR THE COMMANDER OF THE FAITHFUL!
A CARROT FOR THE COMMANDER OF THE FAITHFUL!
CLAP
A CARROT FOR THE COMMANDER OF THE FAITHFUL!
CLAP
CLAP
IT'S A FAILURE! I WISH I'D NEVER CLAPPED EYES ON YOU!
WAIT A MINUTE! UNLESS YOU'RE LOOKING FOR A BLACK EYE, YOU'D BETTER PAY ME!
LOOKING TO BE PAID? YOU MUST BE JOKING!
JOKING, EH?... LOOK INTO MY EYES!
YOU ARE A POST!
MASTER! MASTER! WAKE UP! THAT'S FUNNY... ANYONE WOULD THINK HE WAS DEAF!
CLAPCLAP CLAPCLAP CLAPCLAP

THE OCCIDENTAL PHILTRE

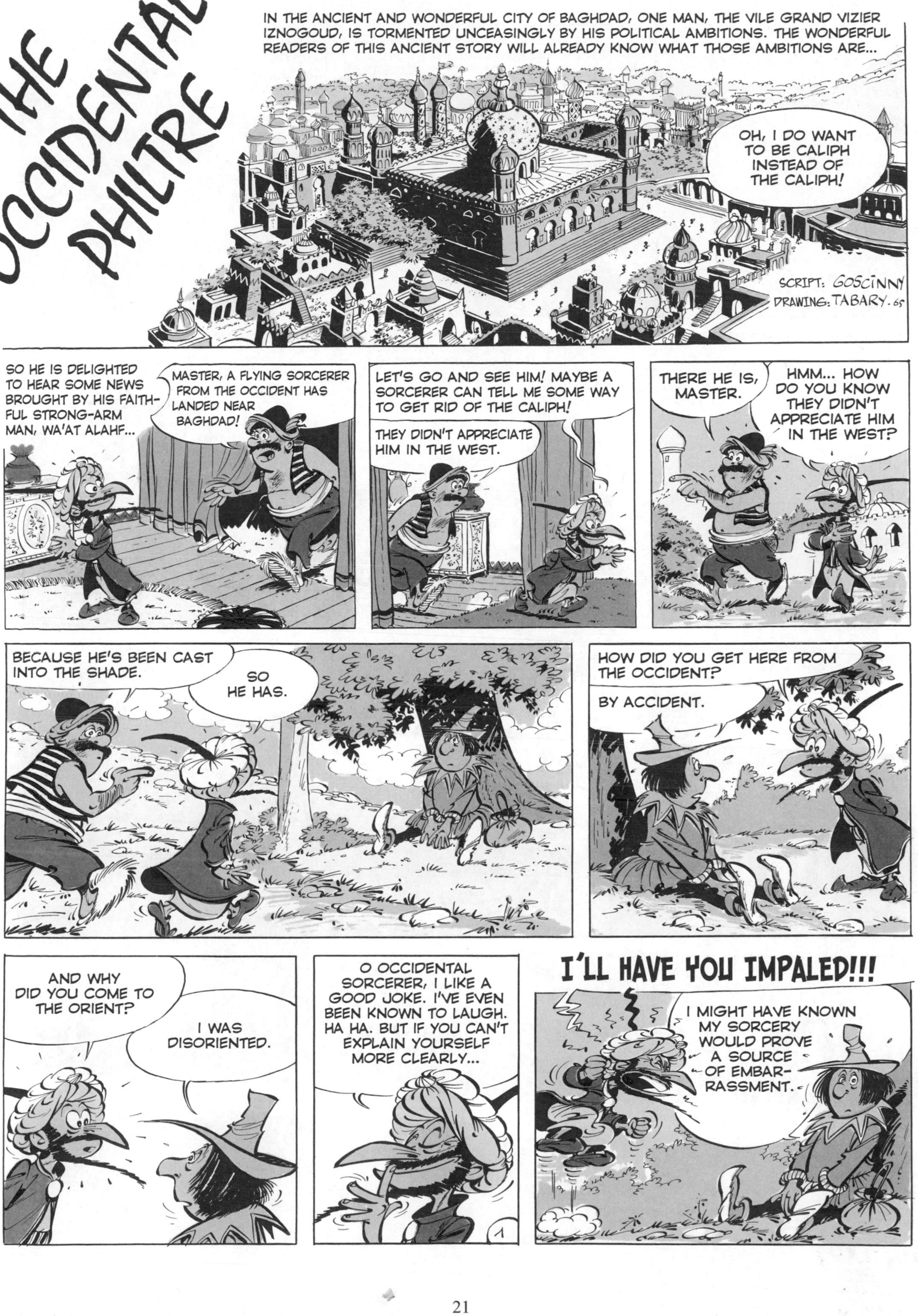

IN THE ANCIENT AND WONDERFUL CITY OF BAGHDAD, ONE MAN, THE VILE GRAND VIZIER IZNOGOUD, IS TORMENTED UNCEASINGLY BY HIS POLITICAL AMBITIONS. THE WONDERFUL READERS OF THIS ANCIENT STORY WILL ALREADY KNOW WHAT THOSE AMBITIONS ARE...
OH, I DO WANT TO BE CALIPH INSTEAD OF THE CALIPH!
SCRIPT: GOSCINNY
DRAWING: TABARY. 65
SO HE IS DELIGHTED TO HEAR SOME NEWS BROUGHT BY HIS FAITHFUL STRONG-ARM MAN, WA'AT ALAHF...
MASTER, A FLYING SORCERER FROM THE OCCIDENT HAS LANDED NEAR BAGHDAD!
LET'S GO AND SEE HIM! MAYBE A SORCERER CAN TELL ME SOME WAY TO GET RID OF THE CALIPH!
THEY DIDN'T APPRECIATE HIM IN THE WEST.
THERE HE IS, MASTER.
HMM... HOW DO YOU KNOW THEY DIDN'T APPRECIATE HIM IN THE WEST?
BECAUSE HE'S BEEN CAST INTO THE SHADE.
SO HE HAS.
HOW DID YOU GET HERE FROM THE OCCIDENT?
BY ACCIDENT.
AND WHY DID YOU COME TO THE ORIENT?
I WAS DISORIENTED.
O OCCIDENTAL SORCERER, I LIKE A GOOD JOKE. I'VE EVEN BEEN KNOWN TO LAUGH. HA HA. BUT IF YOU CAN'T EXPLAIN YOURSELF MORE CLEARLY...
I'LL HAVE YOU IMPALED!!!
I MIGHT HAVE KNOWN MY SORCERY WOULD PROVE A SOURCE OF EMBARRASSMENT.
1

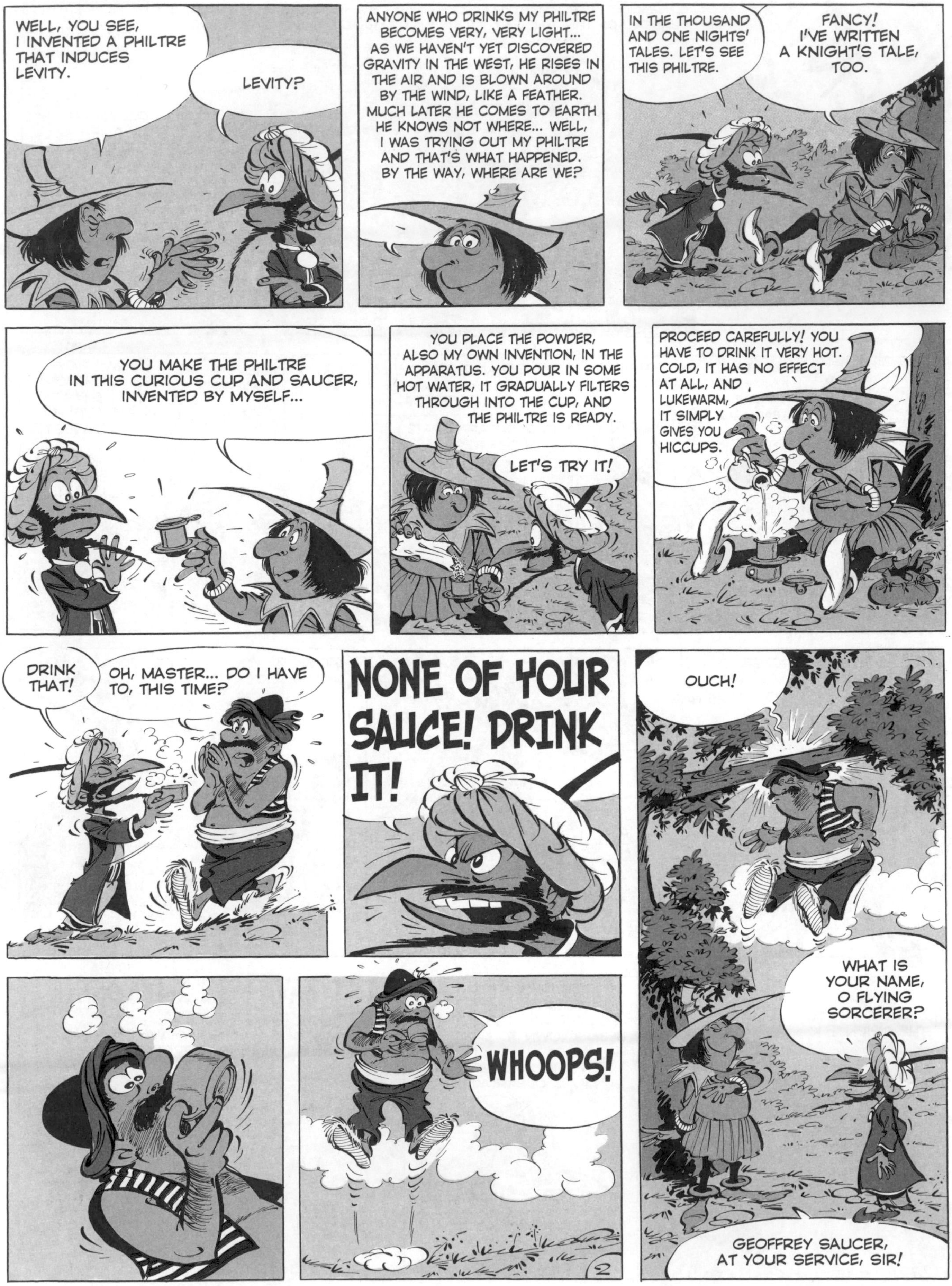
WELL, YOU SEE, I INVENTED A PHILTRE THAT INDUCES LEVITY.
LEVITY?
ANYONE WHO DRINKS MY PHILTRE BECOMES VERY, VERY LIGHT... AS WE HAVEN'T YET DISCOVERED GRAVITY IN THE WEST, HE RISES IN THE AIR AND IS BLOWN AROUND BY THE WIND, LIKE A FEATHER. MUCH LATER HE COMES TO EARTH HE KNOWS NOT WHERE... WELL, I WAS TRYING OUT MY PHILTRE AND THAT'S WHAT HAPPENED. BY THE WAY, WHERE ARE WE?
IN THE THOUSAND AND ONE NIGHTS' TALES. LET'S SEE THIS PHILTRE.
FANCY! I'VE WRITTEN A KNIGHT'S TALE, TOO.
YOU MAKE THE PHILTRE IN THIS CURIOUS CUP AND SAUCER, INVENTED BY MYSELF...
YOU PLACE THE POWDER, ALSO MY OWN INVENTION, IN THE APPARATUS. YOU POUR IN SOME HOT WATER, IT GRADUALLY FILTERS THROUGH INTO THE CUP, AND THE PHILTRE IS READY.
LET'S TRY IT!
PROCEED CAREFULLY! YOU HAVE TO DRINK IT VERY HOT. COLD, IT HAS NO EFFECT AT ALL, AND LUKEWARM, IT SIMPLY GIVES YOU HICCUPS.
DRINK THAT!
OH, MASTER... DO I HAVE TO, THIS TIME?
NONE OF YOUR SAUCE! DRINK IT!
OUCH!
WHOOPS!
WHAT IS YOUR NAME, O FLYING SORCERER?
GEOFFREY SAUCER, AT YOUR SERVICE, SIR!

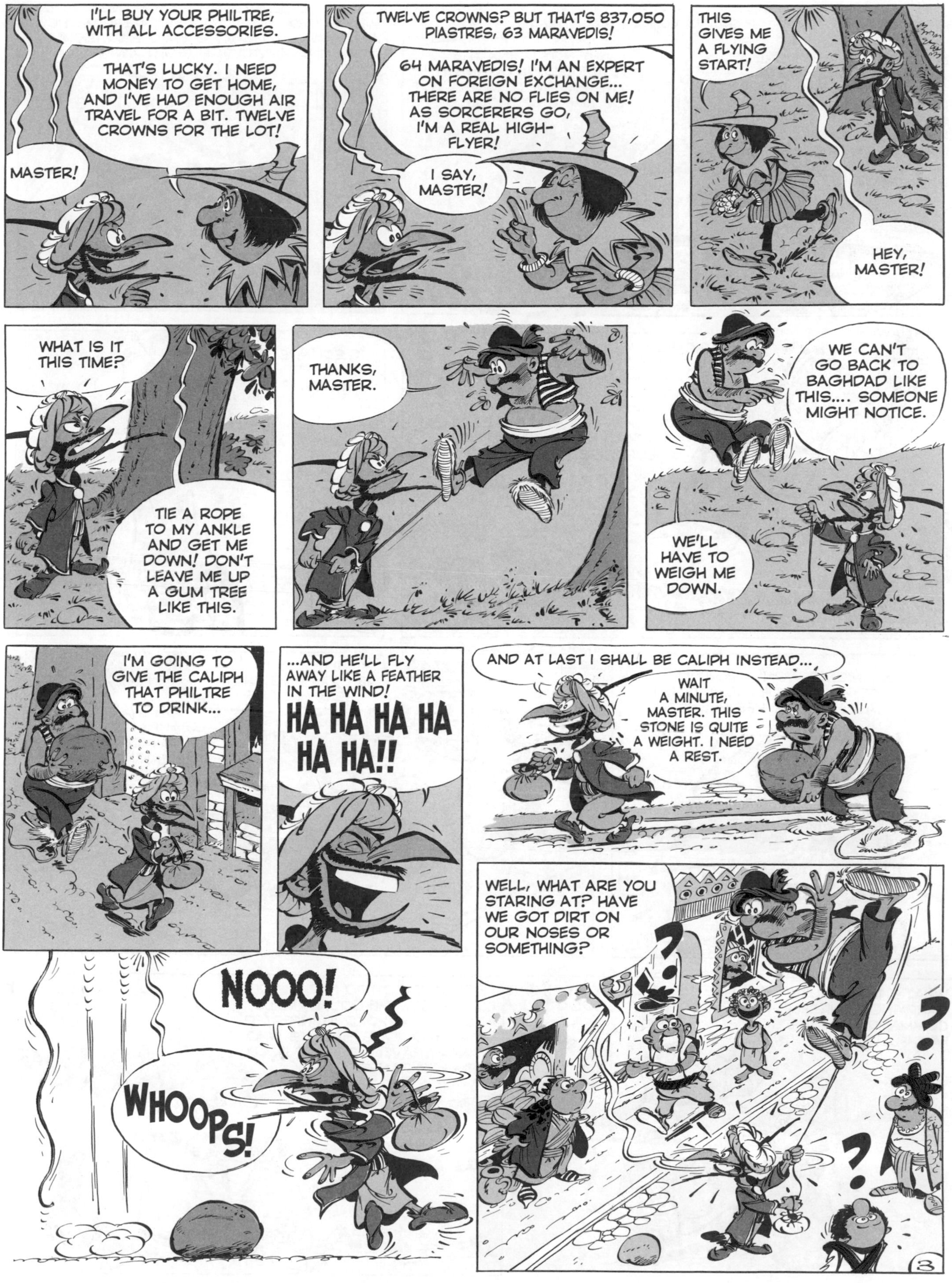
I'LL BUY YOUR PHILTRE, WITH ALL ACCESSORIES.
THAT'S LUCKY. I NEED MONEY TO GET HOME, AND I'VE HAD ENOUGH AIR TRAVEL FOR A BIT. TWELVE CROWNS FOR THE LOT!
MASTER!
TWELVE CROWNS? BUT THAT'S 837,050 PIASTRES, 63 MARAVEDIS!
64 MARAVEDIS! I'M AN EXPERT ON FOREIGN EXCHANGE... THERE ARE NO FLIES ON ME! AS SORCERERS GO, I'M A REAL HIGH-FLYER!
I SAY, MASTER!
THIS GIVES ME A FLYING START!
HEY, MASTER!
WHAT IS IT THIS TIME?
TIE A ROPE TO MY ANKLE AND GET ME DOWN! DON'T LEAVE ME UP A GUM TREE LIKE THIS.
THANKS, MASTER.
WE CAN'T GO BACK TO BAGHDAD LIKE THIS.... SOMEONE MIGHT NOTICE.
WE'LL HAVE TO WEIGH ME DOWN.
I'M GOING TO GIVE THE CALIPH THAT PHILTRE TO DRINK...
...AND HE'LL FLY AWAY LIKE A FEATHER IN THE WIND!
HA HA HA HA HA HA!!
AND AT LAST I SHALL BE CALIPH INSTEAD...
WAIT A MINUTE, MASTER. THIS STONE IS QUITE A WEIGHT. I NEED A REST.
NOOO!
WHOOPS!
WELL, WHAT ARE YOU STARING AT? HAVE WE GOT DIRT ON OUR NOSES OR SOMETHING?
?
?
?
3

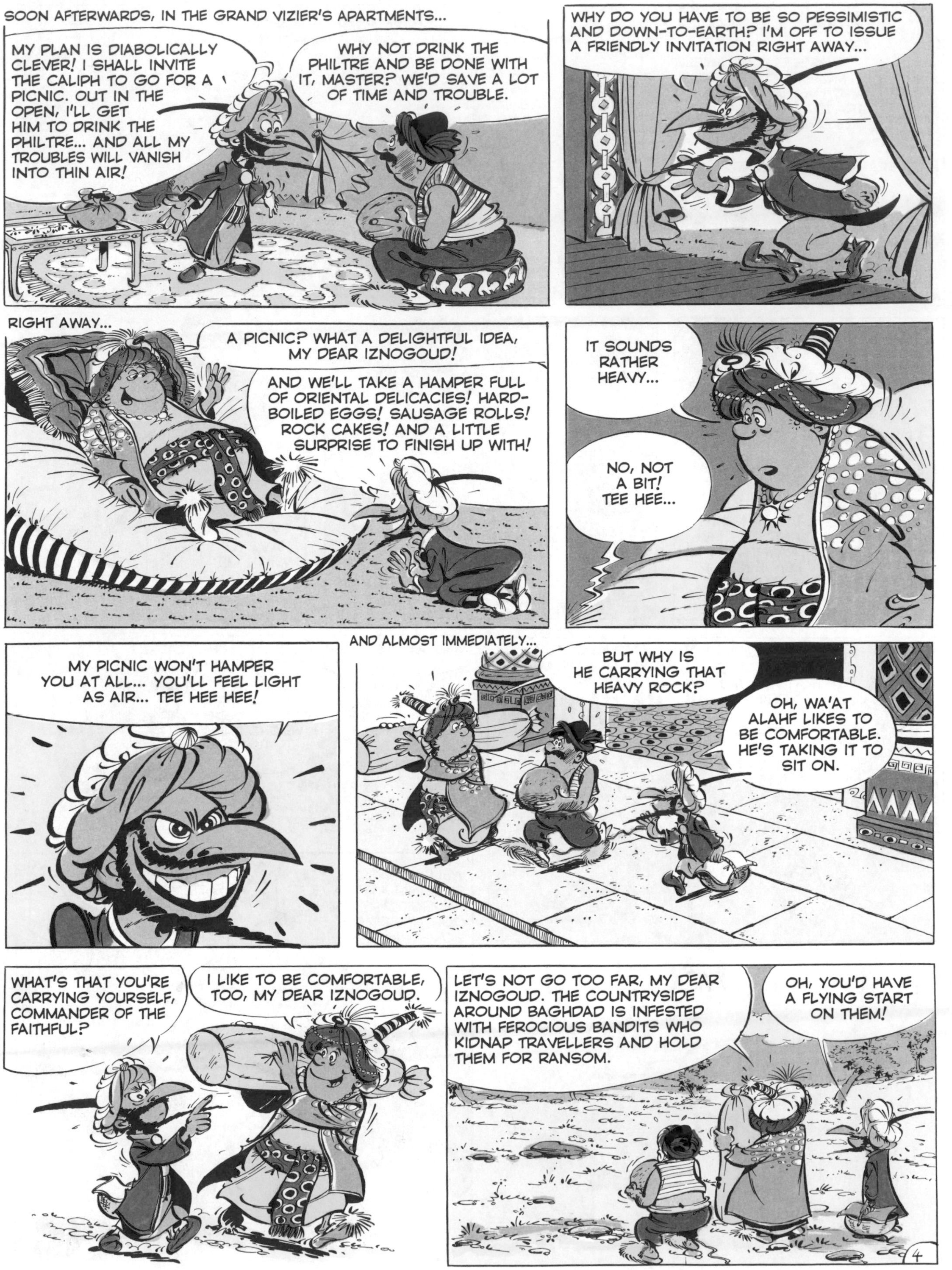

SOON AFTERWARDS, IN THE GRAND VIZIER'S APARTMENTS...
MY PLAN IS DIABOLICALLY CLEVER! I SHALL INVITE THE CALIPH TO GO FOR A PICNIC. OUT IN THE OPEN, I'LL GET HIM TO DRINK THE PHILTRE... AND ALL MY TROUBLES WILL VANISH INTO THIN AIR!
WHY NOT DRINK THE PHILTRE AND BE DONE WITH IT, MASTER? WE'D SAVE A LOT OF TIME AND TROUBLE.
WHY DO YOU HAVE TO BE SO PESSIMISTIC AND DOWN-TO-EARTH? I'M OFF TO ISSUE A FRIENDLY INVITATION RIGHT AWAY...
RIGHT AWAY...
A PICNIC? WHAT A DELIGHTFUL IDEA, MY DEAR IZNOGOUD!
AND WE'LL TAKE A HAMPER FULL OF ORIENTAL DELICACIES! HARD-BOILED EGGS! SAUSAGE ROLLS! ROCK CAKES! AND A LITTLE SURPRISE TO FINISH UP WITH!
IT SOUNDS RATHER HEAVY...
NO, NOT A BIT! TEE HEE...
MY PICNIC WON'T HAMPER YOU AT ALL... YOU'LL FEEL LIGHT AS AIR... TEE HEE HEE!
AND ALMOST IMMEDIATELY...
BUT WHY IS HE CARRYING THAT HEAVY ROCK?
OH, WA'AT ALAHF LIKES TO BE COMFORTABLE. HE'S TAKING IT TO SIT ON.
WHAT'S THAT YOU'RE CARRYING YOURSELF, COMMANDER OF THE FAITHFUL?
I LIKE TO BE COMFORTABLE, TOO, MY DEAR IZNOGOUD.
LET'S NOT GO TOO FAR, MY DEAR IZNOGOUD. THE COUNTRYSIDE AROUND BAGHDAD IS INFESTED WITH FEROCIOUS BANDITS WHO KIDNAP TRAVELLERS AND HOLD THEM FOR RANSOM.
OH, YOU'D HAVE A FLYING START ON THEM!
4

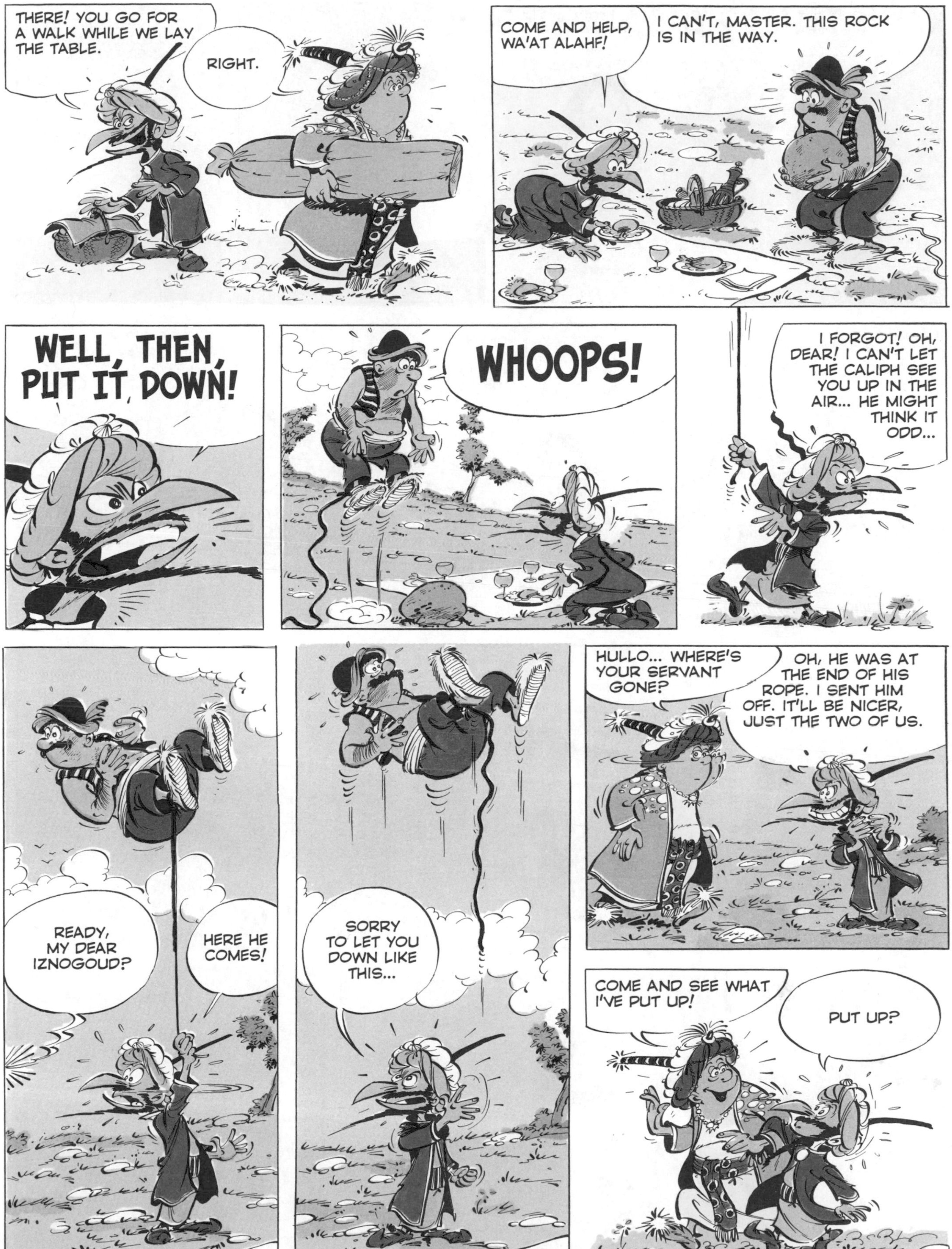

THERE! YOU GO FOR A WALK WHILE WE LAY THE TABLE.
RIGHT.
COME AND HELP, WA'AT ALAHF!
I CAN'T, MASTER. THIS ROCK IS IN THE WAY.
WELL, THEN, PUT IT DOWN!
WHOOPS!
I FORGOT! OH, DEAR! I CAN'T LET THE CALIPH SEE YOU UP IN THE AIR... HE MIGHT THINK IT ODD...
READY, MY DEAR IZNOGOUD?
HERE HE COMES!
SORRY TO LET YOU DOWN LIKE THIS...
HULLO... WHERE'S YOUR SERVANT GONE?
OH, HE WAS AT THE END OF HIS ROPE. I SENT HIM OFF. IT'LL BE NICER, JUST THE TWO OF US.
COME AND SEE WHAT I'VE PUT UP!
PUT UP?
5

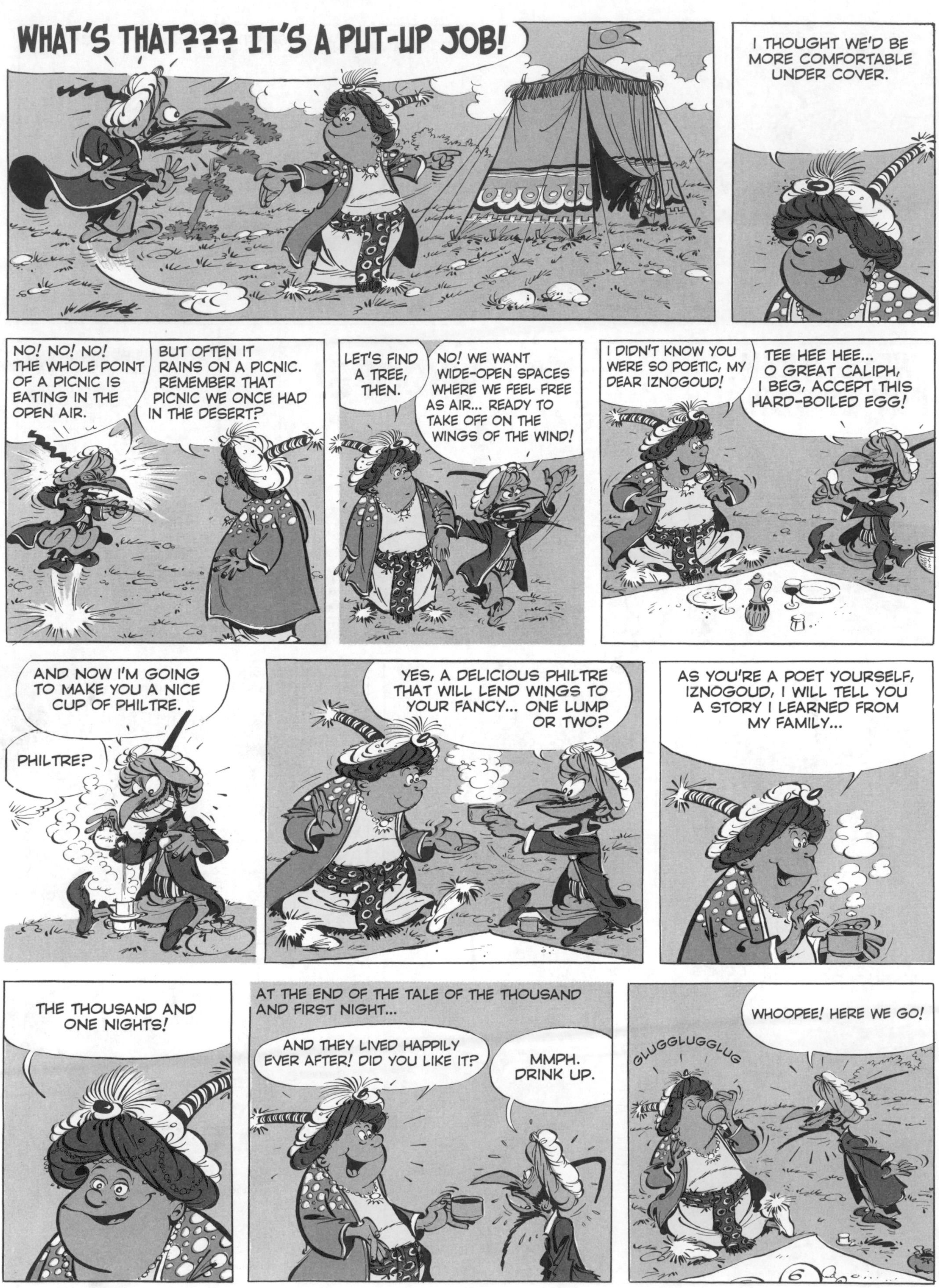
WHAT'S THAT??? IT'S A PUT-UP JOB!
I THOUGHT WE'D BE MORE COMFORTABLE UNDER COVER.
NO! NO! NO! THE WHOLE POINT OF A PICNIC IS EATING IN THE OPEN AIR.
BUT OFTEN IT RAINS ON A PICNIC. REMEMBER THAT PICNIC WE ONCE HAD IN THE DESERT?
LET'S FIND A TREE, THEN.
NO! WE WANT WIDE-OPEN SPACES WHERE WE FEEL FREE AS AIR... READY TO TAKE OFF ON THE WINGS OF THE WIND!
I DIDN'T KNOW YOU WERE SO POETIC, MY DEAR IZNOGOUD!
TEE HEE HEE... O GREAT CALIPH, I BEG, ACCEPT THIS HARD-BOILED EGG!
AND NOW I'M GOING TO MAKE YOU A NICE CUP OF PHILTRE.
PHILTRE?
YES, A DELICIOUS PHILTRE THAT WILL LEND WINGS TO YOUR FANCY... ONE LUMP OR TWO?
AS YOU'RE A POET YOURSELF, IZNOGOUD, I WILL TELL YOU A STORY I LEARNED FROM MY FAMILY...
THE THOUSAND AND ONE NIGHTS!
AT THE END OF THE TALE OF THE THOUSAND AND FIRST NIGHT...
AND THEY LIVED HAPPILY EVER AFTER! DID YOU LIKE IT?
MMPH. DRINK UP.
GLUGGLUGGLUG
WHOOPEE! HERE WE GO!

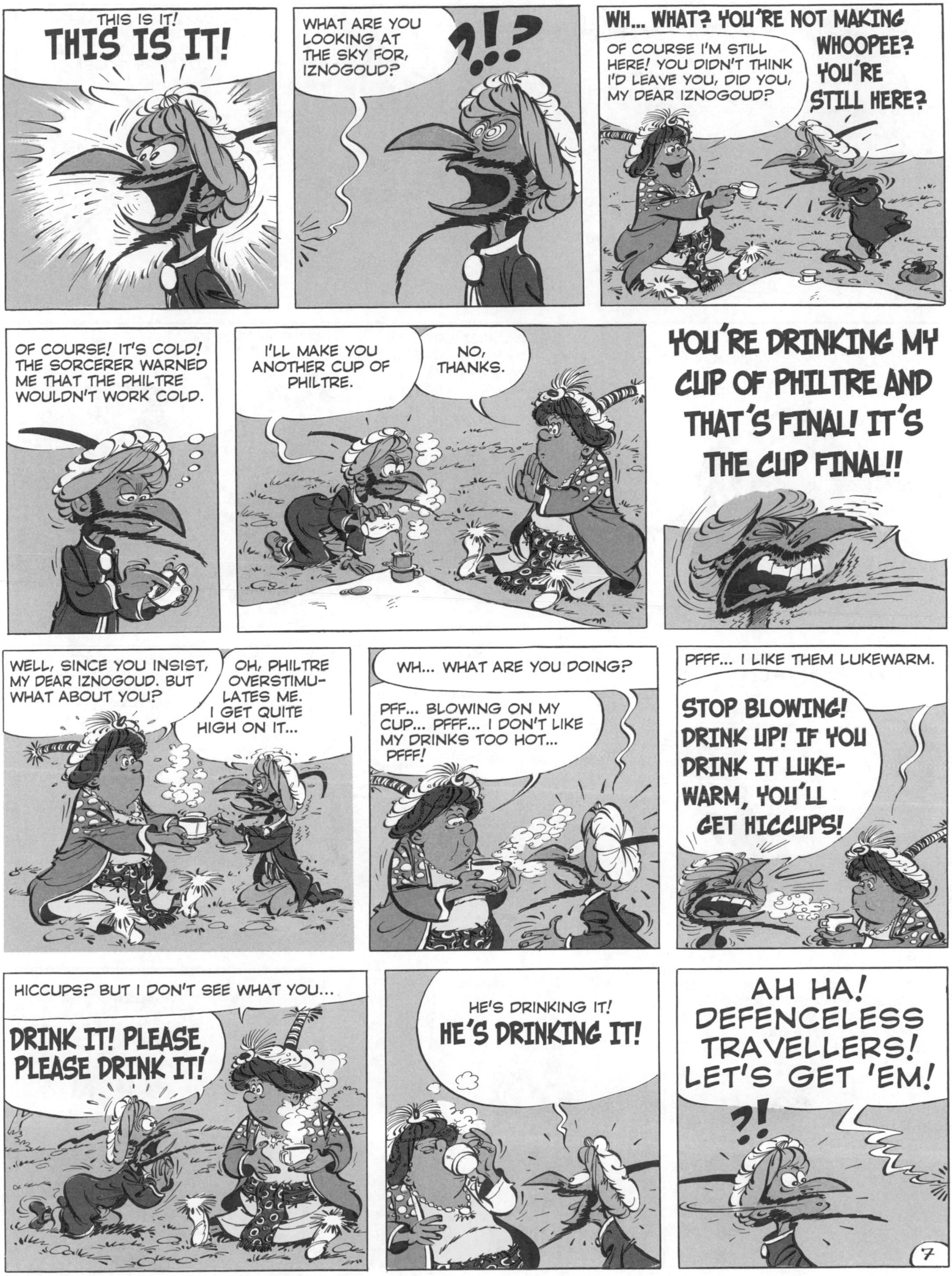
THIS IS IT!
THIS IS IT!
WHAT ARE YOU LOOKING AT THE SKY FOR, IZNOGOUD?
?!?
WH... WHAT? YOU'RE NOT MAKING WHOOPEE? YOU'RE STILL HERE?
OF COURSE I'M STILL HERE! YOU DIDN'T THINK I'D LEAVE YOU, DID YOU, MY DEAR IZNOGOUD?
OF COURSE! IT'S COLD! THE SORCERER WARNED ME THAT THE PHILTRE WOULDN'T WORK COLD.
I'LL MAKE YOU ANOTHER CUP OF PHILTRE.
NO, THANKS.
YOU'RE DRINKING MY CUP OF PHILTRE AND THAT'S FINAL! IT'S THE CUP FINAL!!
WELL, SINCE YOU INSIST, MY DEAR IZNOGOUD. BUT WHAT ABOUT YOU?
OH, PHILTRE OVERSTIMU-LATES ME. I GET QUITE HIGH ON IT...
WH... WHAT ARE YOU DOING?
PFF... BLOWING ON MY CUP... PFFF... I DON'T LIKE MY DRINKS TOO HOT... PFFF!
PFFF... I LIKE THEM LUKEWARM.
STOP BLOWING! DRINK UP! IF YOU DRINK IT LUKE-WARM, YOU'LL GET HICCUPS!
HICCUPS? BUT I DON'T SEE WHAT YOU...
DRINK IT! PLEASE, PLEASE DRINK IT!
HE'S DRINKING IT!
HE'S DRINKING IT!
AH HA! DEFENCELESS TRAVELLERS! LET'S GET 'EM!
?!
7

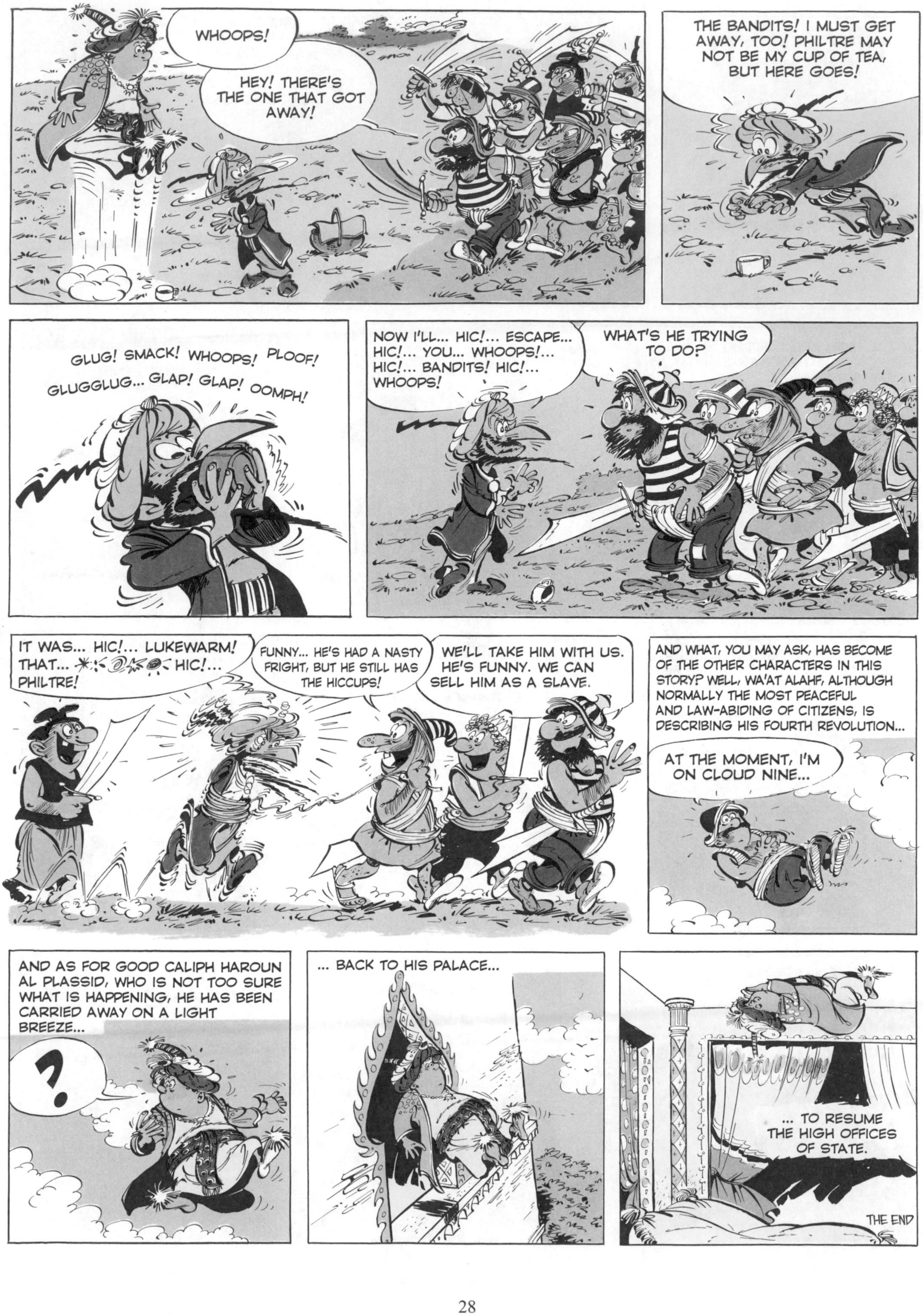
WHOOPS!
HEY! THERE'S THE ONE THAT GOT AWAY!
THE BANDITS! I MUST GET AWAY, TOO! PHILTRE MAY NOT BE MY CUP OF TEA, BUT HERE GOES!
GLUG! SMACK! WHOOPS! PLOOF!
GLUGGLUG... GLAP! GLAP! OOMPH!
NOW I'LL... HIC!... ESCAPE... HIC!... YOU... WHOOPS!... HIC!... BANDITS! HIC!... WHOOPS!
WHAT'S HE TRYING TO DO?
IT WAS... HIC!... LUKEWARM! THAT... HIC!... PHILTRE!
FUNNY... HE'S HAD A NASTY FRIGHT, BUT HE STILL HAS THE HICCUPS!
WE'LL TAKE HIM WITH US. HE'S FUNNY. WE CAN SELL HIM AS A SLAVE.
AND WHAT, YOU MAY ASK, HAS BECOME OF THE OTHER CHARACTERS IN THIS STORY? WELL, WA'AT ALAHF, ALTHOUGH NORMALLY THE MOST PEACEFUL AND LAW-ABIDING OF CITIZENS, IS DESCRIBING HIS FOURTH REVOLUTION...
AT THE MOMENT, I'M ON CLOUD NINE...
AND AS FOR GOOD CALIPH HAROUN AL PLASSID, WHO IS NOT TOO SURE WHAT IS HAPPENING, HE HAS BEEN CARRIED AWAY ON A LIGHT BREEZE...
?
... BACK TO HIS PALACE...
... TO RESUME THE HIGH OFFICES OF STATE.
THE END

THE TIME MACHINE

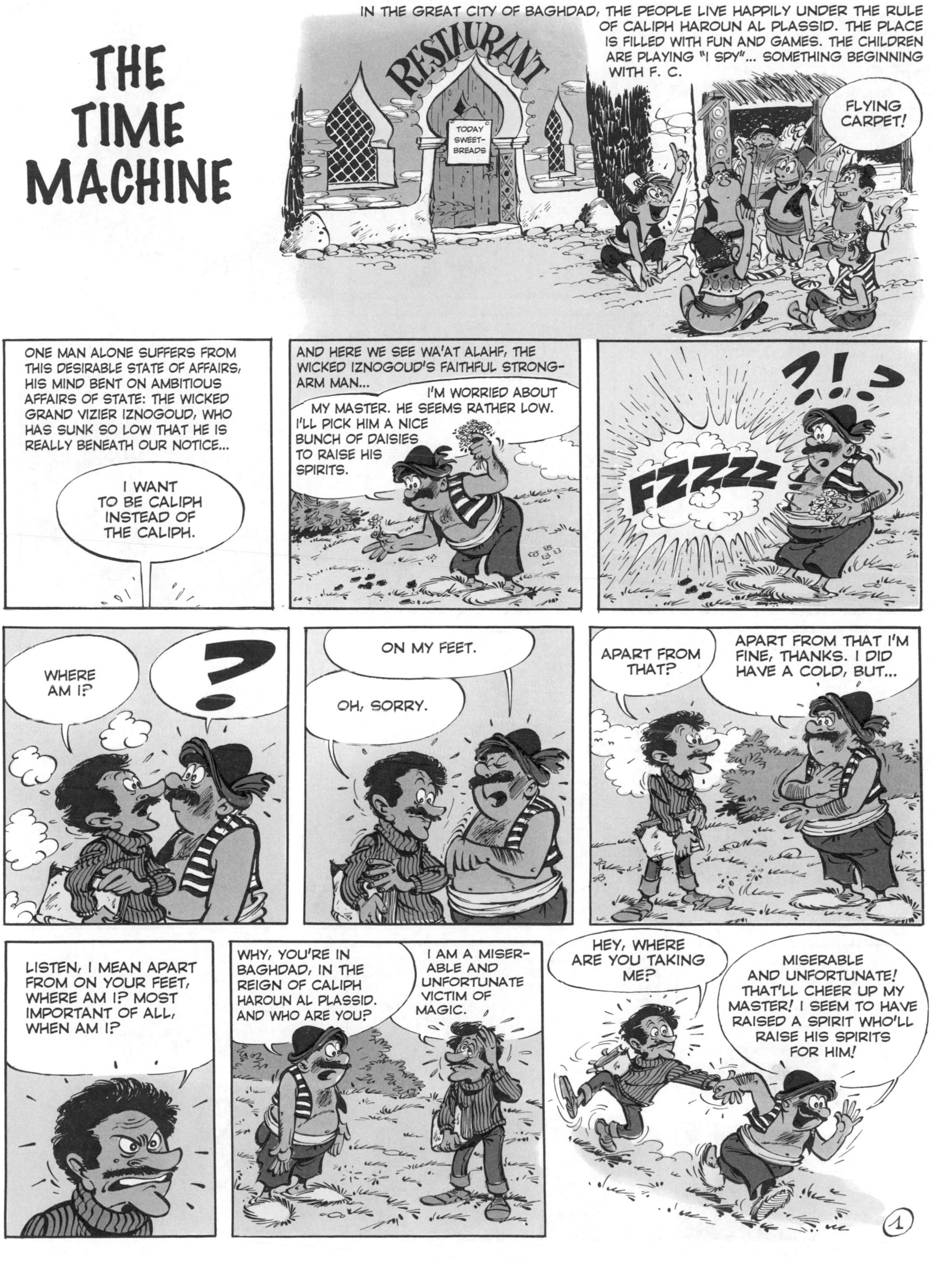
IN THE GREAT CITY OF BAGHDAD, THE PEOPLE LIVE HAPPILY UNDER THE RULE OF CALIPH HAROUN AL PLASSID. THE PLACE IS FILLED WITH FUN AND GAMES. THE CHILDREN ARE PLAYING "I SPY"... SOMETHING BEGINNING WITH F. C.
RESTAURANT
TODAY SWEET-BREADS
FLYING CARPET!
ONE MAN ALONE SUFFERS FROM THIS DESIRABLE STATE OF AFFAIRS, HIS MIND BENT ON AMBITIOUS AFFAIRS OF STATE: THE WICKED GRAND VIZIER IZNOGOUD, WHO HAS SUNK SO LOW THAT HE IS REALLY BENEATH OUR NOTICE...
I WANT TO BE CALIPH INSTEAD OF THE CALIPH.
AND HERE WE SEE WA'AT ALAHF, THE WICKED IZNOGOUD'S FAITHFUL STRONG-ARM MAN...
I'M WORRIED ABOUT MY MASTER. HE SEEMS RATHER LOW. I'LL PICK HIM A NICE BUNCH OF DAISIES TO RAISE HIS SPIRITS.
?!?
FZZZZ
WHERE AM I?
?
ON MY FEET.
OH, SORRY.
APART FROM THAT?
APART FROM THAT I'M FINE, THANKS. I DID HAVE A COLD, BUT...
LISTEN, I MEAN APART FROM ON YOUR FEET, WHERE AM I? MOST IMPORTANT OF ALL, WHEN AM I?
WHY, YOU'RE IN BAGHDAD, IN THE REIGN OF CALIPH HAROUN AL PLASSID. AND WHO ARE YOU?
I AM A MISER-ABLE AND UNFORTUNATE VICTIM OF MAGIC.
HEY, WHERE ARE YOU TAKING ME?
MISERABLE AND UNFORTUNATE! THAT'LL CHEER UP MY MASTER! I SEEM TO HAVE RAISED A SPIRIT WHO'LL RAISE HIS SPIRITS FOR HIM!
1

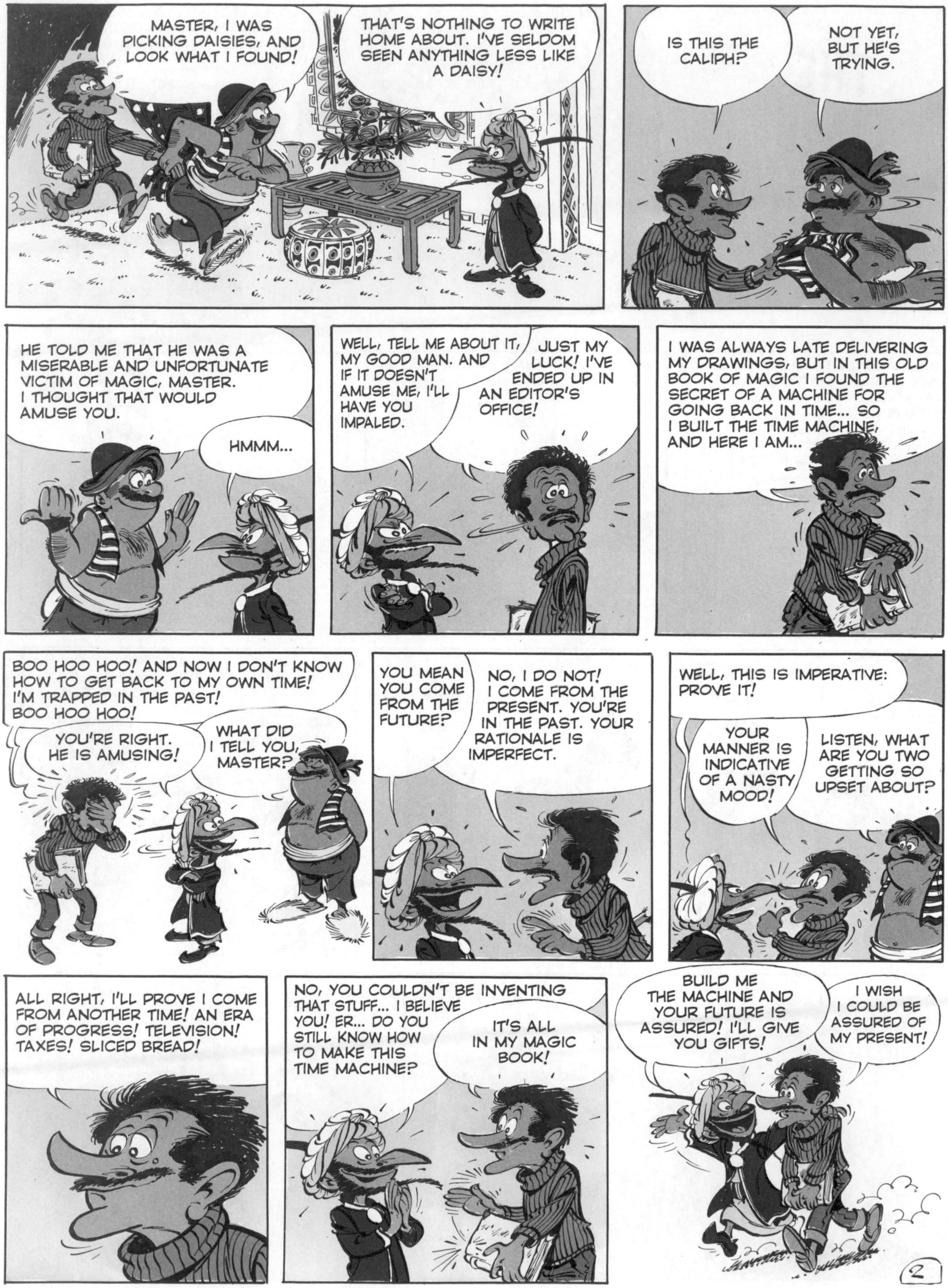
MASTER, I WAS PICKING DAISIES, AND LOOK WHAT I FOUND!
THAT'S NOTHING TO WRITE HOME ABOUT. I'VE SELDOM SEEN ANYTHING LESS LIKE A DAISY!
IS THIS THE CALIPH?
NOT YET, BUT HE'S TRYING.
HE TOLD ME THAT HE WAS A MISERABLE AND UNFORTUNATE VICTIM OF MAGIC, MASTER. I THOUGHT THAT WOULD AMUSE YOU.
HMMM...
WELL, TELL ME ABOUT IT, MY GOOD MAN. AND IF IT DOESN'T AMUSE ME, I'LL HAVE YOU IMPALED.
JUST MY LUCK! I'VE ENDED UP IN AN EDITOR'S OFFICE!
I WAS ALWAYS LATE DELIVERING MY DRAWINGS, BUT IN THIS OLD BOOK OF MAGIC I FOUND THE SECRET OF A MACHINE FOR GOING BACK IN TIME... SO I BUILT THE TIME MACHINE, AND HERE I AM...
BOO HOO HOO! AND NOW I DON'T KNOW HOW TO GET BACK TO MY OWN TIME! I'M TRAPPED IN THE PAST! BOO HOO HOO!
YOU'RE RIGHT. HE IS AMUSING!
WHAT DID I TELL YOU, MASTER?
YOU MEAN YOU COME FROM THE FUTURE?
NO, I DO NOT! I COME FROM THE PRESENT. YOU'RE IN THE PAST. YOUR RATIONALE IS IMPERFECT.
WELL, THIS IS IMPERATIVE: PROVE IT!
YOUR MANNER IS INDICATIVE OF A NASTY MOOD!
LISTEN, WHAT ARE YOU TWO GETTING SO UPSET ABOUT?
ALL RIGHT, I'LL PROVE I COME FROM ANOTHER TIME! AN ERA OF PROGRESS! TELEVISION! TAXES! SLICED BREAD!
NO, YOU COULDN'T BE INVENTING THAT STUFF... I BELIEVE YOU! ER... DO YOU STILL KNOW HOW TO MAKE THIS TIME MACHINE?
IT'S ALL IN MY MAGIC BOOK!
BUILD ME THE MACHINE AND YOUR FUTURE IS ASSURED! I'LL GIVE YOU GIFTS!
I WISH I COULD BE ASSURED OF MY PRESENT!
2

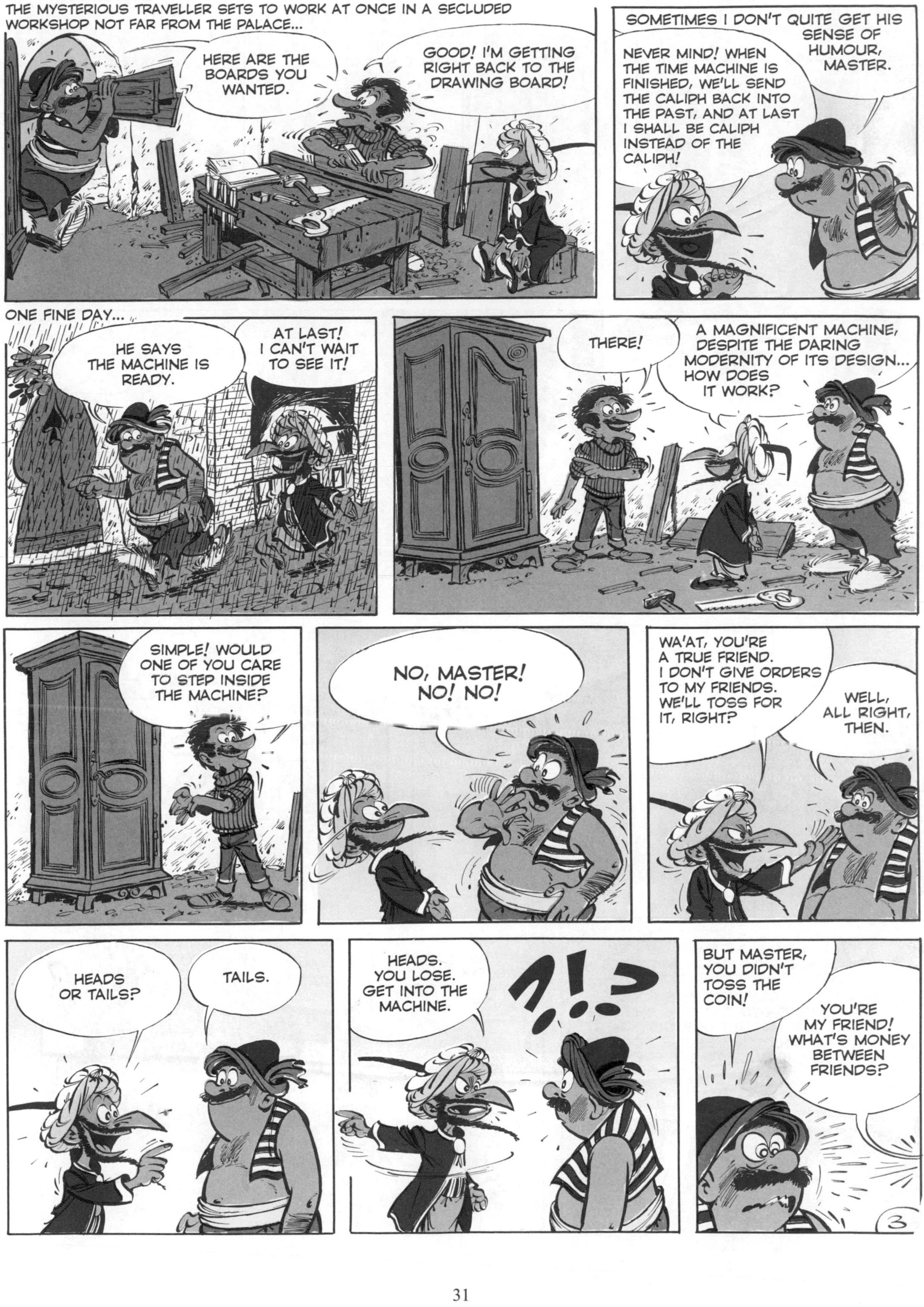
THE MYSTERIOUS TRAVELLER SETS TO WORK AT ONCE IN A SECLUDED WORKSHOP NOT FAR FROM THE PALACE...
HERE ARE THE BOARDS YOU WANTED.
GOOD! I'M GETTING RIGHT BACK TO THE DRAWING BOARD!
SOMETIMES I DON'T QUITE GET HIS SENSE OF HUMOUR, MASTER.
NEVER MIND! WHEN THE TIME MACHINE IS FINISHED, WE'LL SEND THE CALIPH BACK INTO THE PAST, AND AT LAST I SHALL BE CALIPH INSTEAD OF THE CALIPH!
ONE FINE DAY...
HE SAYS THE MACHINE IS READY.
AT LAST! I CAN'T WAIT TO SEE IT!
THERE!
A MAGNIFICENT MACHINE, DESPITE THE DARING MODERNITY OF ITS DESIGN... HOW DOES IT WORK?
SIMPLE! WOULD ONE OF YOU CARE TO STEP INSIDE THE MACHINE?
NO, MASTER! NO! NO!
WA'AT, YOU'RE A TRUE FRIEND. I DON'T GIVE ORDERS TO MY FRIENDS. WE'LL TOSS FOR IT, RIGHT?
WELL, ALL RIGHT, THEN.
HEADS OR TAILS?
TAILS.
HEADS. YOU LOSE. GET INTO THE MACHINE.
?!?
BUT MASTER, YOU DIDN'T TOSS THE COIN!
YOU'RE MY FRIEND! WHAT'S MONEY BETWEEN FRIENDS?
3

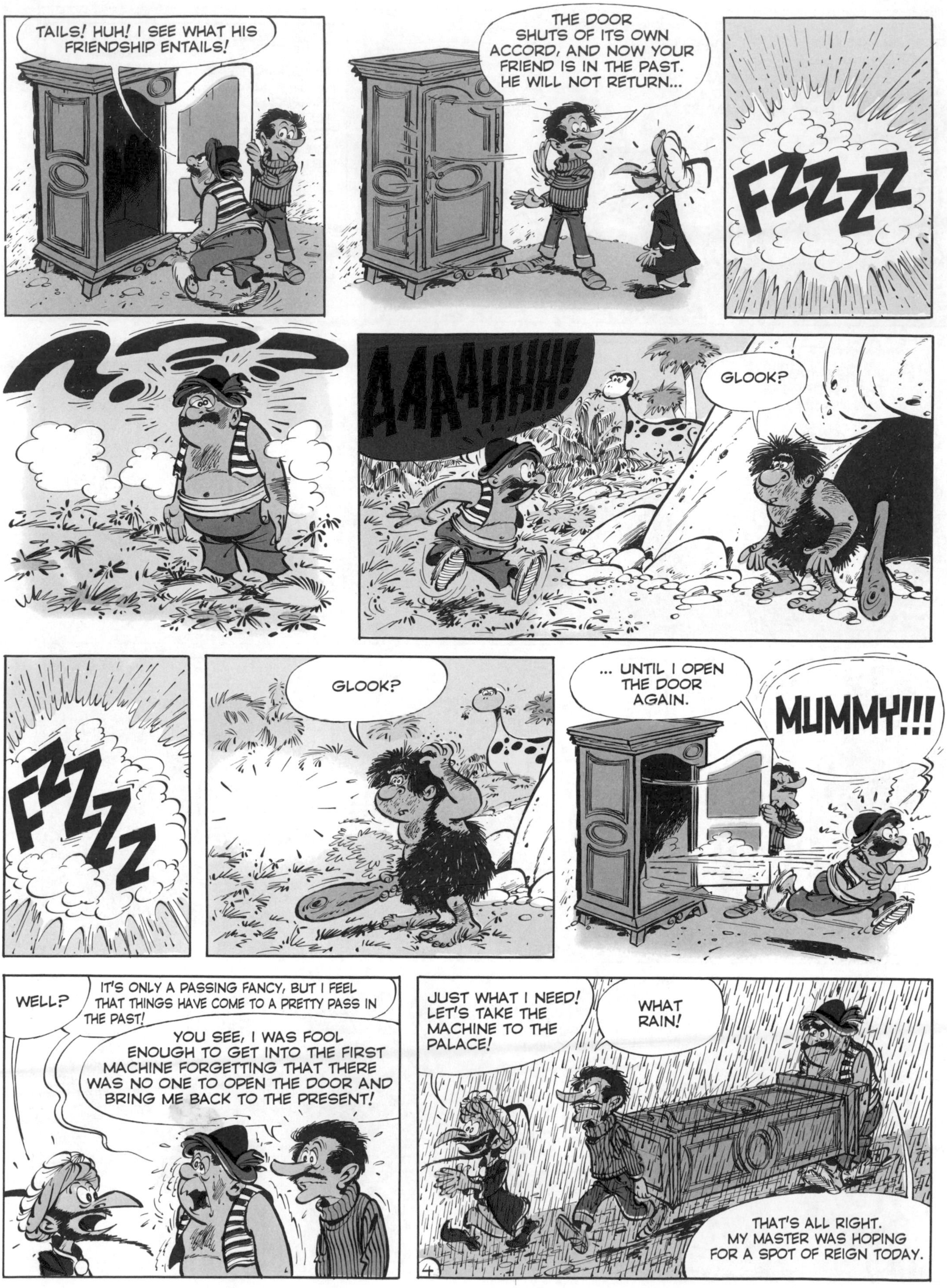
TAILS! HUH! I SEE WHAT HIS FRIENDSHIP ENTAILS!
THE DOOR SHUTS OF ITS OWN ACCORD, AND NOW YOUR FRIEND IS IN THE PAST. HE WILL NOT RETURN...
FZZZZ
?.?.?
AAAAHHH!
GLOOK?
FZZZZ
GLOOK?
... UNTIL I OPEN THE DOOR AGAIN.
MUMMY!!!
WELL?
IT'S ONLY A PASSING FANCY, BUT I FEEL THAT THINGS HAVE COME TO A PRETTY PASS IN THE PAST!
YOU SEE, I WAS FOOL ENOUGH TO GET INTO THE FIRST MACHINE FORGETTING THAT THERE WAS NO ONE TO OPEN THE DOOR AND BRING ME BACK TO THE PRESENT!
JUST WHAT I NEED! LET'S TAKE THE MACHINE TO THE PALACE!
WHAT RAIN!
THAT'S ALL RIGHT. MY MASTER WAS HOPING FOR A SPOT OF REIGN TODAY.

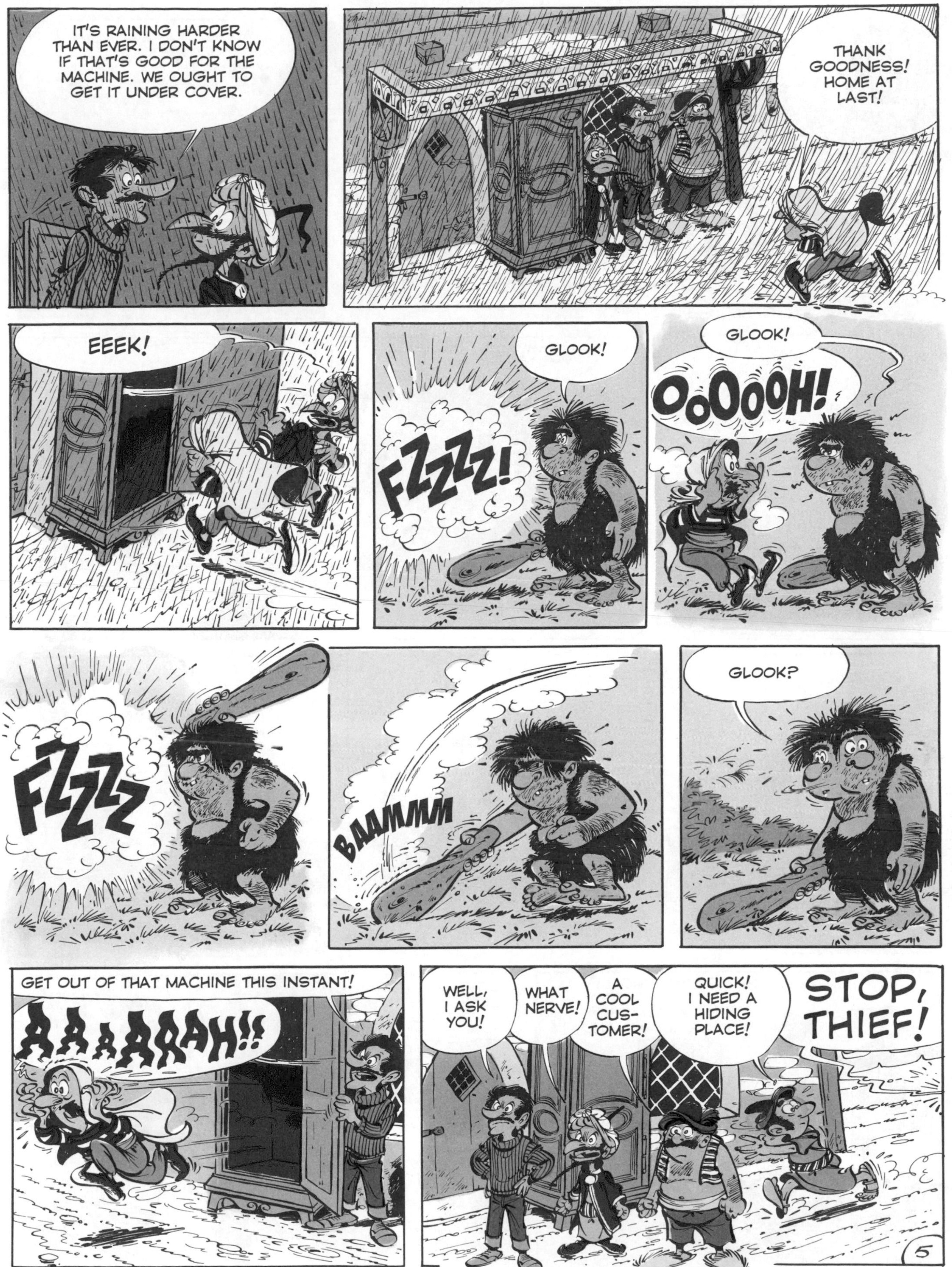

IT'S RAINING HARDER THAN EVER. I DON'T KNOW IF THAT'S GOOD FOR THE MACHINE. WE OUGHT TO GET IT UNDER COVER.
THANK GOODNESS! HOME AT LAST!
EEEK!
GLOOK!
FZZZZ!
GLOOK!
OOOOOH!
FZZZZ
BAAMMM
GLOOK?
GET OUT OF THAT MACHINE THIS INSTANT!
AAAARAH!!
WELL, I ASK YOU!
WHAT NERVE!
A COOL CUS-TOMER!
QUICK! I NEED A HIDING PLACE!
STOP, THIEF!
5

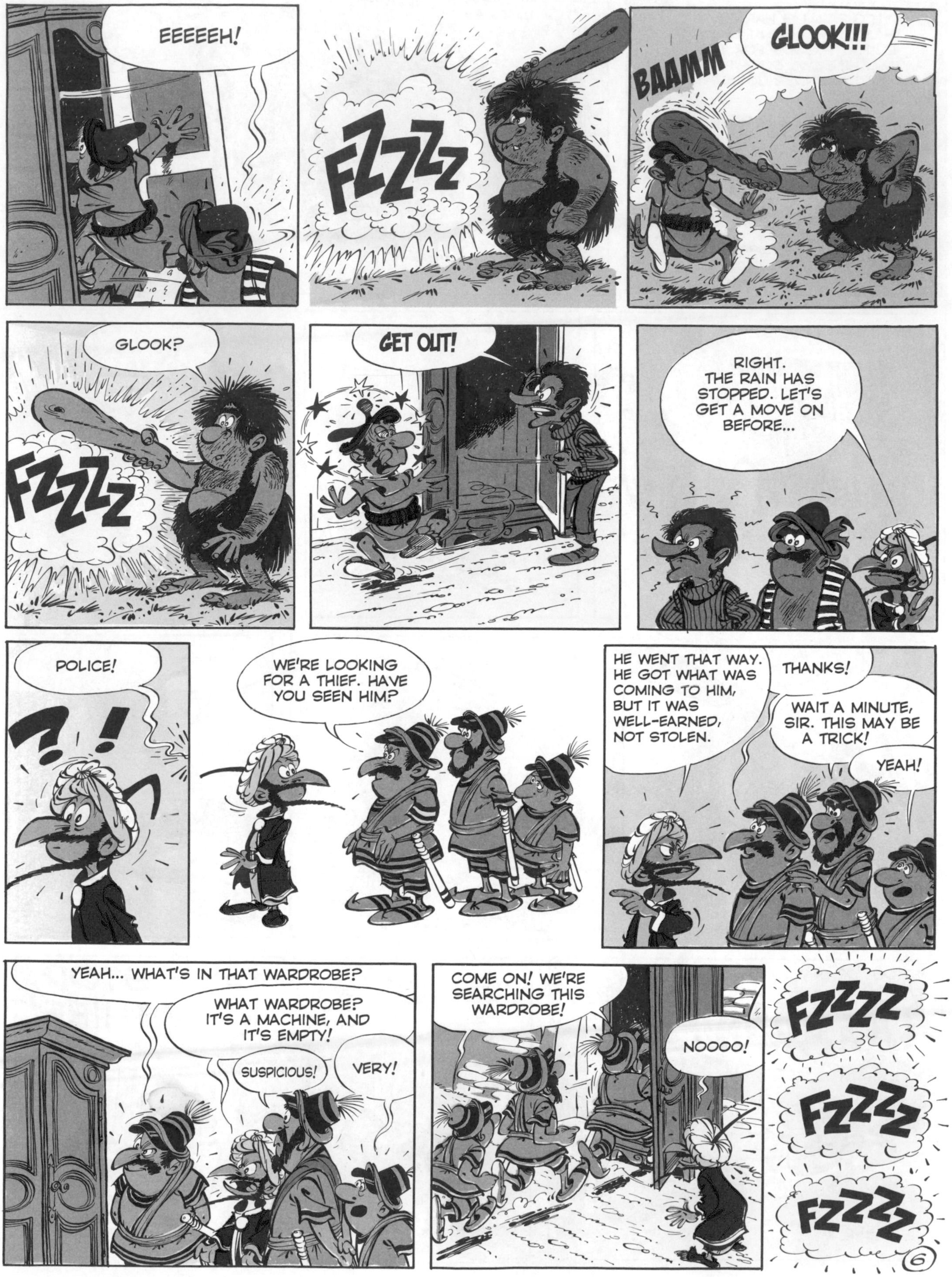
EEEEEH!
FZZZZ
BAAMM
GLOOK!!!
GLOOK?
FZZZZ
GET OUT!
RIGHT. THE RAIN HAS STOPPED. LET'S GET A MOVE ON BEFORE...
POLICE!
?!
WE'RE LOOKING FOR A THIEF. HAVE YOU SEEN HIM?
HE WENT THAT WAY. HE GOT WHAT WAS COMING TO HIM, BUT IT WAS WELL-EARNED, NOT STOLEN.
THANKS!
WAIT A MINUTE, SIR. THIS MAY BE A TRICK!
YEAH!
YEAH... WHAT'S IN THAT WARDROBE?
WHAT WARDROBE? IT'S A MACHINE, AND IT'S EMPTY!
SUSPICIOUS!
VERY!
COME ON! WE'RE SEARCHING THIS WARDROBE!
NOOOO!
FZZZZ
FZZZZ
FZZZZ
6

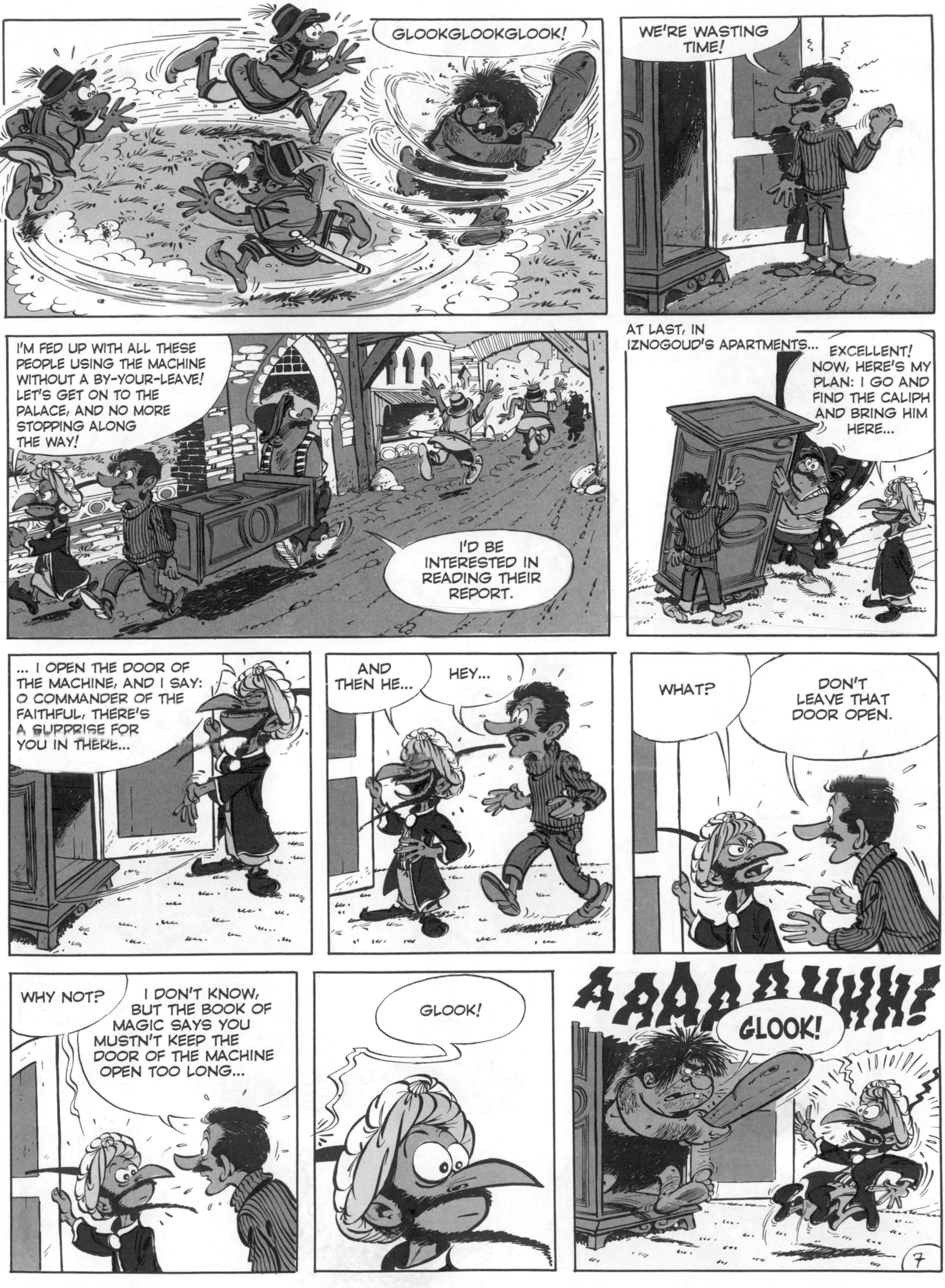
GLOOKGLOOKGLOOK!
WE'RE WASTING TIME!
I'M FED UP WITH ALL THESE PEOPLE USING THE MACHINE WITHOUT A BY-YOUR-LEAVE! LET'S GET ON TO THE PALACE, AND NO MORE STOPPING ALONG THE WAY!
I'D BE INTERESTED IN READING THEIR REPORT.
AT LAST, IN IZNOGOUD'S APARTMENTS...
EXCELLENT! NOW, HERE'S MY PLAN: I GO AND FIND THE CALIPH AND BRING HIM HERE...
... I OPEN THE DOOR OF THE MACHINE, AND I SAY: O COMMANDER OF THE FAITHFUL, THERE'S A SURPRISE FOR YOU IN THERE...
AND THEN HE...
HEY...
WHAT?
DON'T LEAVE THAT DOOR OPEN.
WHY NOT?
I DON'T KNOW, BUT THE BOOK OF MAGIC SAYS YOU MUSTN'T KEEP THE DOOR OF THE MACHINE OPEN TOO LONG...
GLOOK!
AAAAAHH!
GLOOK!
7

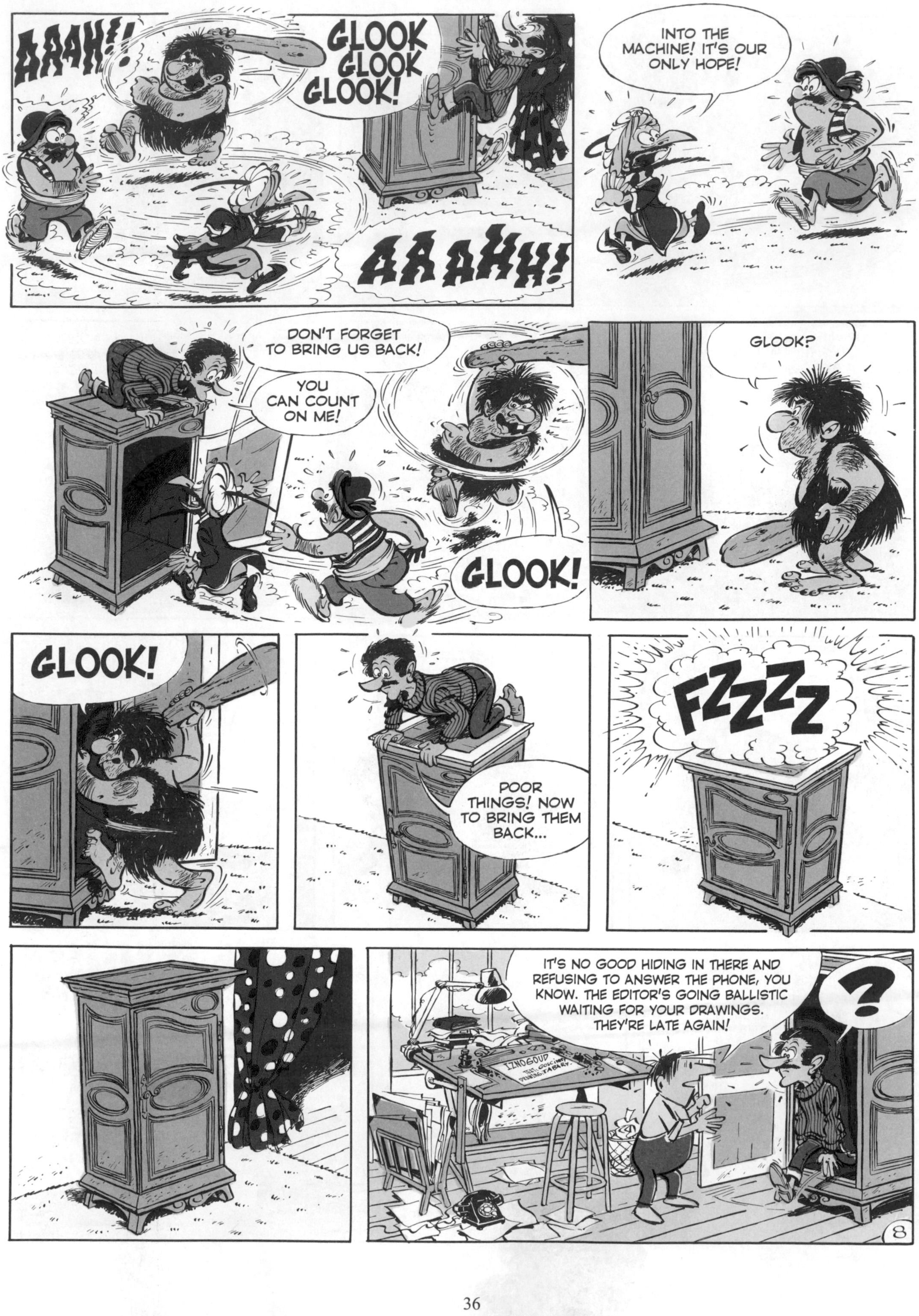
AAAH!!
GLOOK GLOOK GLOOK!
AAAHH!
INTO THE MACHINE! IT'S OUR ONLY HOPE!
DON'T FORGET TO BRING US BACK!
YOU CAN COUNT ON ME!
GLOOK!
GLOOK?
GLOOK!
POOR THINGS! NOW TO BRING THEM BACK...
FZZZZ
IT'S NO GOOD HIDING IN THERE AND REFUSING TO ANSWER THE PHONE, YOU KNOW. THE EDITOR'S GOING BALLISTIC WAITING FOR YOUR DRAWINGS. THEY'RE LATE AGAIN!
?
8

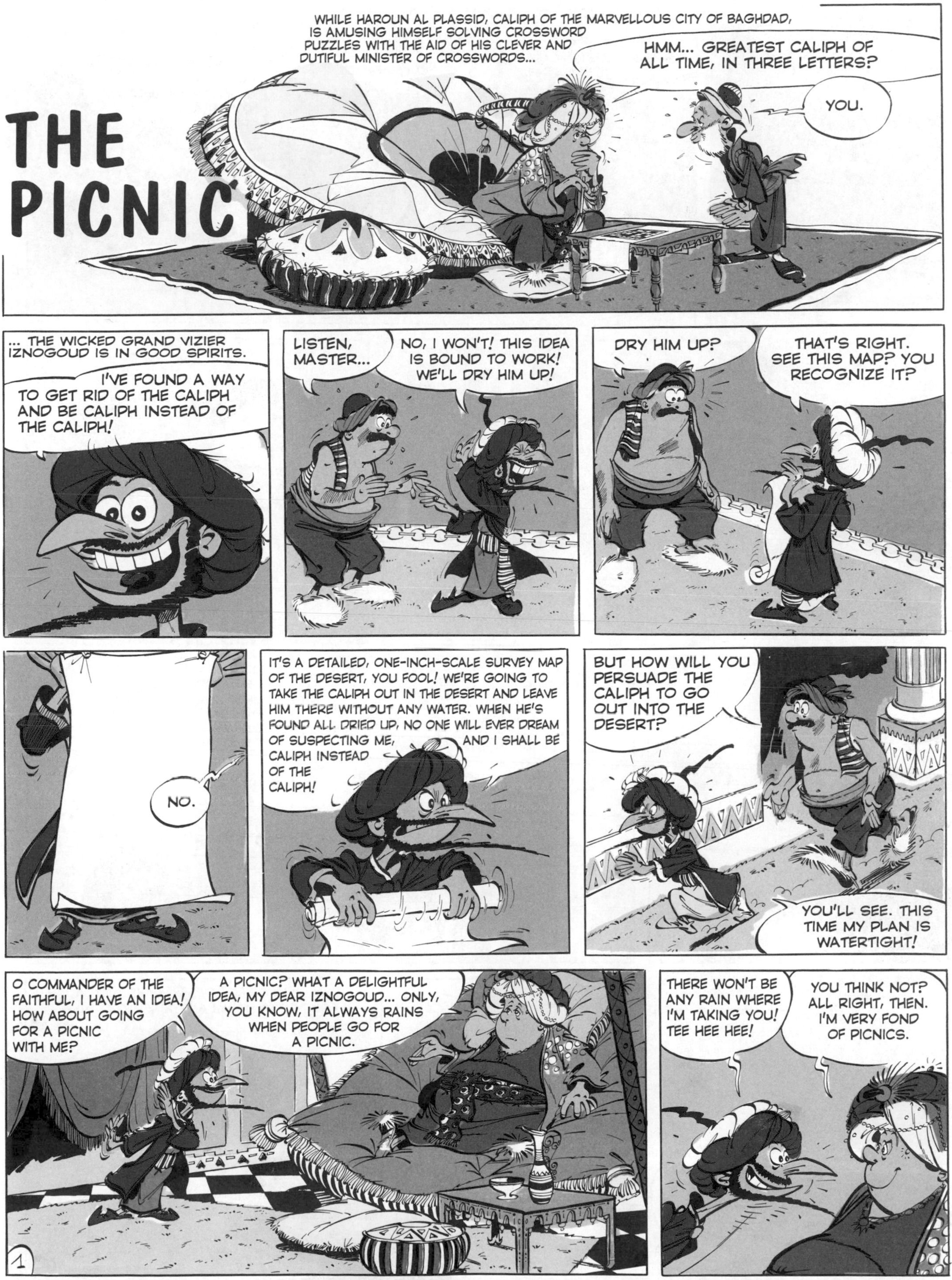
THE PICNIC
WHILE HAROUN AL PLASSID, CALIPH OF THE MARVELLOUS CITY OF BAGHDAD, IS AMUSING HIMSELF SOLVING CROSSWORD PUZZLES WITH THE AID OF HIS CLEVER AND DUTIFUL MINISTER OF CROSSWORDS...
HMM... GREATEST CALIPH OF ALL TIME, IN THREE LETTERS?
YOU.
... THE WICKED GRAND VIZIER IZNOGOUD IS IN GOOD SPIRITS.
I'VE FOUND A WAY TO GET RID OF THE CALIPH AND BE CALIPH INSTEAD OF THE CALIPH!
LISTEN, MASTER...
NO, I WON'T! THIS IDEA IS BOUND TO WORK! WE'LL DRY HIM UP!
DRY HIM UP?
THAT'S RIGHT. SEE THIS MAP? YOU RECOGNIZE IT?
NO.
IT'S A DETAILED, ONE-INCH-SCALE SURVEY MAP OF THE DESERT, YOU FOOL! WE'RE GOING TO TAKE THE CALIPH OUT IN THE DESERT AND LEAVE HIM THERE WITHOUT ANY WATER. WHEN HE'S FOUND ALL DRIED UP, NO ONE WILL EVER DREAM OF SUSPECTING ME,
AND I SHALL BE CALIPH INSTEAD OF THE CALIPH!
BUT HOW WILL YOU PERSUADE THE CALIPH TO GO OUT INTO THE DESERT?
YOU'LL SEE. THIS TIME MY PLAN IS WATERTIGHT!
O COMMANDER OF THE FAITHFUL, I HAVE AN IDEA! HOW ABOUT GOING FOR A PICNIC WITH ME?
A PICNIC? WHAT A DELIGHTFUL IDEA, MY DEAR IZNOGOUD... ONLY, YOU KNOW, IT ALWAYS RAINS WHEN PEOPLE GO FOR A PICNIC.
THERE WON'T BE ANY RAIN WHERE I'M TAKING YOU! TEE HEE HEE!
YOU THINK NOT? ALL RIGHT, THEN. I'M VERY FOND OF PICNICS.
1

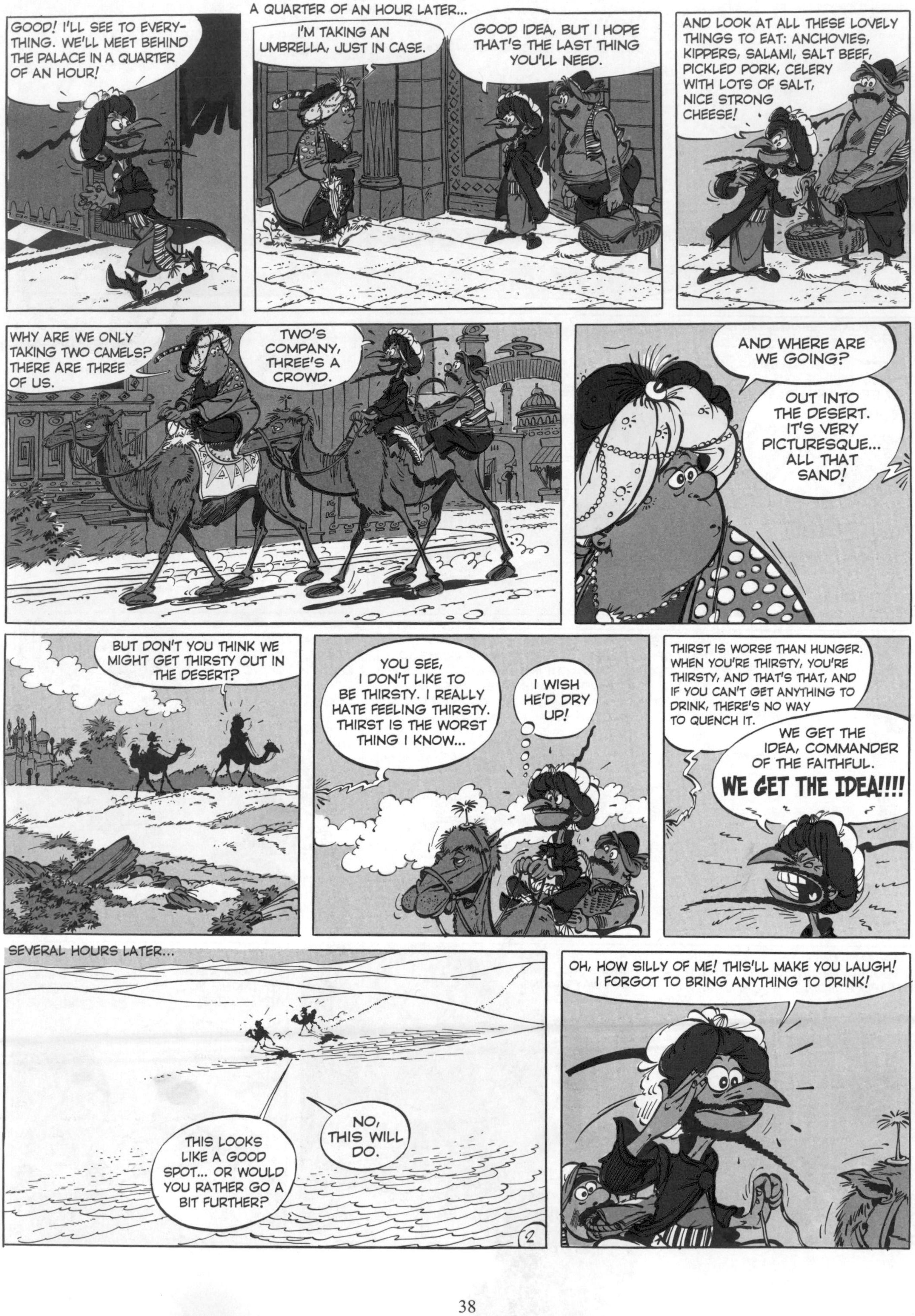
GOOD! I'LL SEE TO EVERYTHING. WE'LL MEET BEHIND THE PALACE IN A QUARTER OF AN HOUR!
A QUARTER OF AN HOUR LATER...
I'M TAKING AN UMBRELLA, JUST IN CASE.
GOOD IDEA, BUT I HOPE THAT'S THE LAST THING YOU'LL NEED.
AND LOOK AT ALL THESE LOVELY THINGS TO EAT: ANCHOVIES, KIPPERS, SALAMI, SALT BEEF, PICKLED PORK, CELERY WITH LOTS OF SALT, NICE STRONG CHEESE!
WHY ARE WE ONLY TAKING TWO CAMELS? THERE ARE THREE OF US.
TWO'S COMPANY, THREE'S A CROWD.
AND WHERE ARE WE GOING?
OUT INTO THE DESERT. IT'S VERY PICTURESQUE... ALL THAT SAND!
BUT DON'T YOU THINK WE MIGHT GET THIRSTY OUT IN THE DESERT?
YOU SEE, I DON'T LIKE TO BE THIRSTY. I REALLY HATE FEELING THIRSTY. THIRST IS THE WORST THING I KNOW...
I WISH HE'D DRY UP!
THIRST IS WORSE THAN HUNGER. WHEN YOU'RE THIRSTY, YOU'RE THIRSTY, AND THAT'S THAT, AND IF YOU CAN'T GET ANYTHING TO DRINK, THERE'S NO WAY TO QUENCH IT.
WE GET THE IDEA, COMMANDER OF THE FAITHFUL.
WE GET THE IDEA!!!!
SEVERAL HOURS LATER...
THIS LOOKS LIKE A GOOD SPOT... OR WOULD YOU RATHER GO A BIT FURTHER?
NO, THIS WILL DO.
OH, HOW SILLY OF ME! THIS'LL MAKE YOU LAUGH! I FORGOT TO BRING ANYTHING TO DRINK!

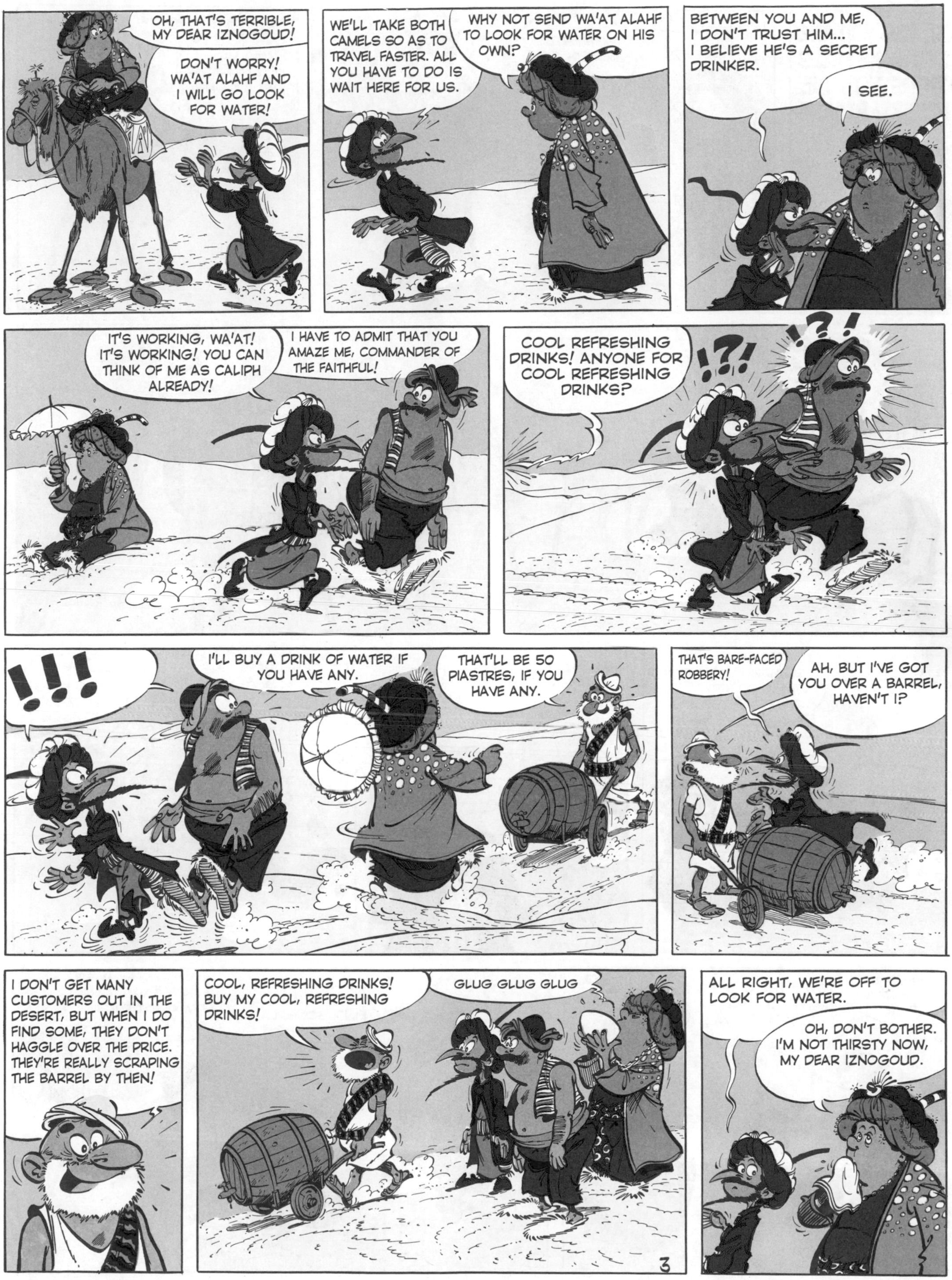
OH, THAT'S TERRIBLE, MY DEAR IZNOGOUD!
DON'T WORRY! WA'AT ALAHF AND I WILL GO LOOK FOR WATER!
WE'LL TAKE BOTH CAMELS SO AS TO TRAVEL FASTER. ALL YOU HAVE TO DO IS WAIT HERE FOR US.
WHY NOT SEND WA'AT ALAHF TO LOOK FOR WATER ON HIS OWN?
BETWEEN YOU AND ME, I DON'T TRUST HIM... I BELIEVE HE'S A SECRET DRINKER.
I SEE.
IT'S WORKING, WA'AT! IT'S WORKING! YOU CAN THINK OF ME AS CALIPH ALREADY!
I HAVE TO ADMIT THAT YOU AMAZE ME, COMMANDER OF THE FAITHFUL!
COOL REFRESHING DRINKS! ANYONE FOR COOL REFRESHING DRINKS?
!?!
!?!
!!!
I'LL BUY A DRINK OF WATER IF YOU HAVE ANY.
THAT'LL BE 50 PIASTRES, IF YOU HAVE ANY.
THAT'S BARE-FACED ROBBERY!
AH, BUT I'VE GOT YOU OVER A BARREL, HAVEN'T I?
I DON'T GET MANY CUSTOMERS OUT IN THE DESERT, BUT WHEN I DO FIND SOME, THEY DON'T HAGGLE OVER THE PRICE. THEY'RE REALLY SCRAPING THE BARREL BY THEN!
COOL, REFRESHING DRINKS! BUY MY COOL, REFRESHING DRINKS!
GLUG GLUG GLUG
3
ALL RIGHT, WE'RE OFF TO LOOK FOR WATER.
OH, DON'T BOTHER. I'M NOT THIRSTY NOW, MY DEAR IZNOGOUD.

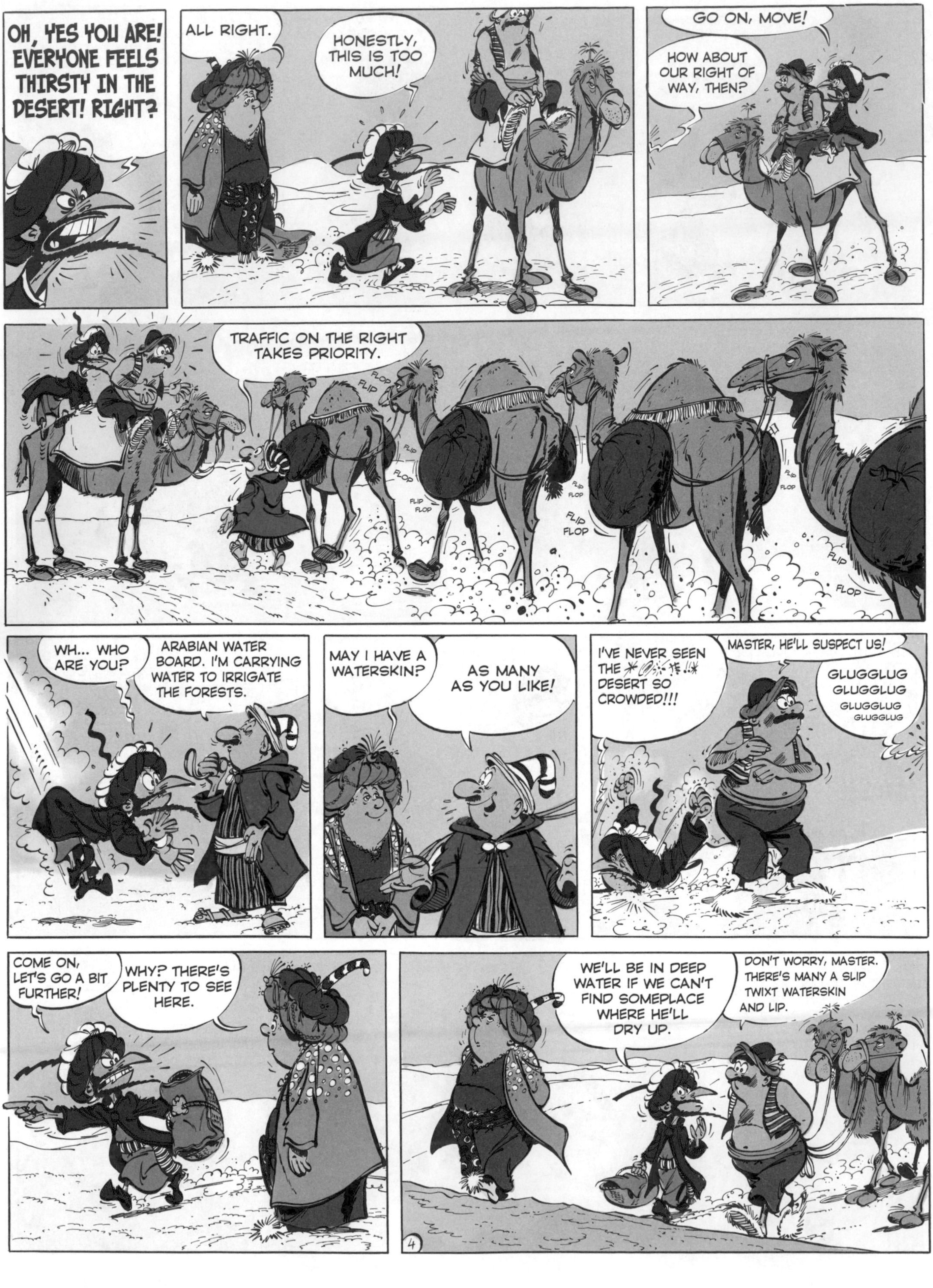
OH, YES YOU ARE! EVERYONE FEELS THIRSTY IN THE DESERT! RIGHT?
ALL RIGHT.
HONESTLY, THIS IS TOO MUCH!
GO ON, MOVE!
HOW ABOUT OUR RIGHT OF WAY, THEN?
TRAFFIC ON THE RIGHT TAKES PRIORITY.
FLOP
FLIP
FLIP
FLOP
FLIP
FLOP
FLIP
FLOP
FLIP
FLOP
FLIP
FLOP
FLIP
FLOP
WH... WHO ARE YOU?
ARABIAN WATER BOARD. I'M CARRYING WATER TO IRRIGATE THE FORESTS.
MAY I HAVE A WATERSKIN?
AS MANY AS YOU LIKE!
I'VE NEVER SEEN THE *@%*!!* DESERT SO CROWDED!!!
MASTER, HE'LL SUSPECT US!
GLUGGLUG
GLUGGLUG
GLUGGLUG
GLUGGLUG
COME ON, LET'S GO A BIT FURTHER!
WHY? THERE'S PLENTY TO SEE HERE.
WE'LL BE IN DEEP WATER IF WE CAN'T FIND SOMEPLACE WHERE HE'LL DRY UP.
DON'T WORRY, MASTER. THERE'S MANY A SLIP TWIXT WATERSKIN AND LIP.
4

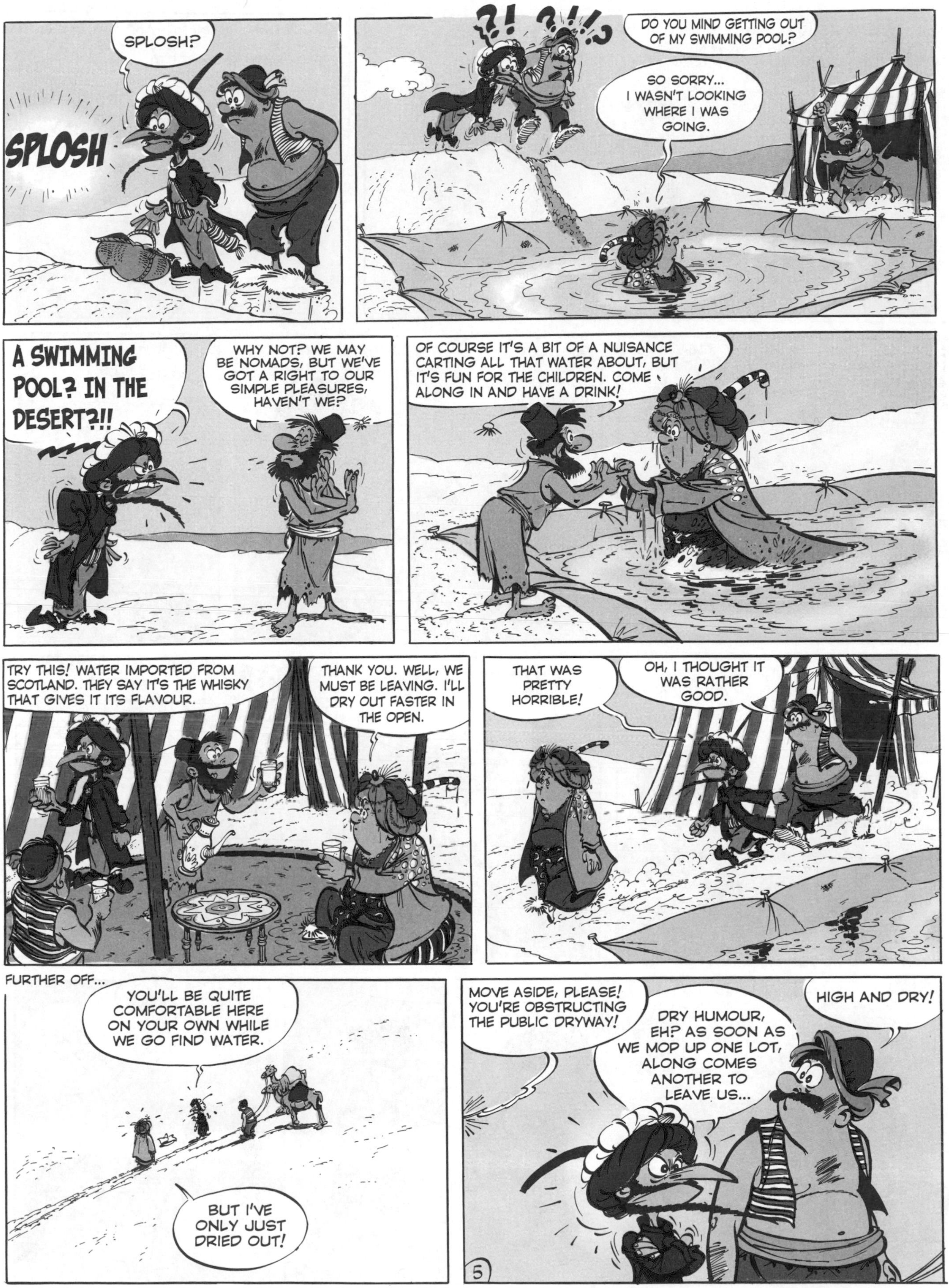

SPLOSH?
SPLOSH
?! ?!!?
DO YOU MIND GETTING OUT OF MY SWIMMING POOL?
SO SORRY... I WASN'T LOOKING WHERE I WAS GOING.
A SWIMMING POOL? IN THE DESERT?!!
WHY NOT? WE MAY BE NOMADS, BUT WE'VE GOT A RIGHT TO OUR SIMPLE PLEASURES, HAVEN'T WE?
OF COURSE IT'S A BIT OF A NUISANCE CARTING ALL THAT WATER ABOUT, BUT IT'S FUN FOR THE CHILDREN. COME ALONG IN AND HAVE A DRINK!
TRY THIS! WATER IMPORTED FROM SCOTLAND. THEY SAY IT'S THE WHISKY THAT GIVES IT ITS FLAVOUR.
THANK YOU. WELL, WE MUST BE LEAVING. I'LL DRY OUT FASTER IN THE OPEN.
THAT WAS PRETTY HORRIBLE!
OH, I THOUGHT IT WAS RATHER GOOD.
FURTHER OFF...
YOU'LL BE QUITE COMFORTABLE HERE ON YOUR OWN WHILE WE GO FIND WATER.
BUT I'VE ONLY JUST DRIED OUT!
MOVE ASIDE, PLEASE! YOU'RE OBSTRUCTING THE PUBLIC DRYWAY!
DRY HUMOUR, EH? AS SOON AS WE MOP UP ONE LOT, ALONG COMES ANOTHER TO LEAVE US...
HIGH AND DRY!
5

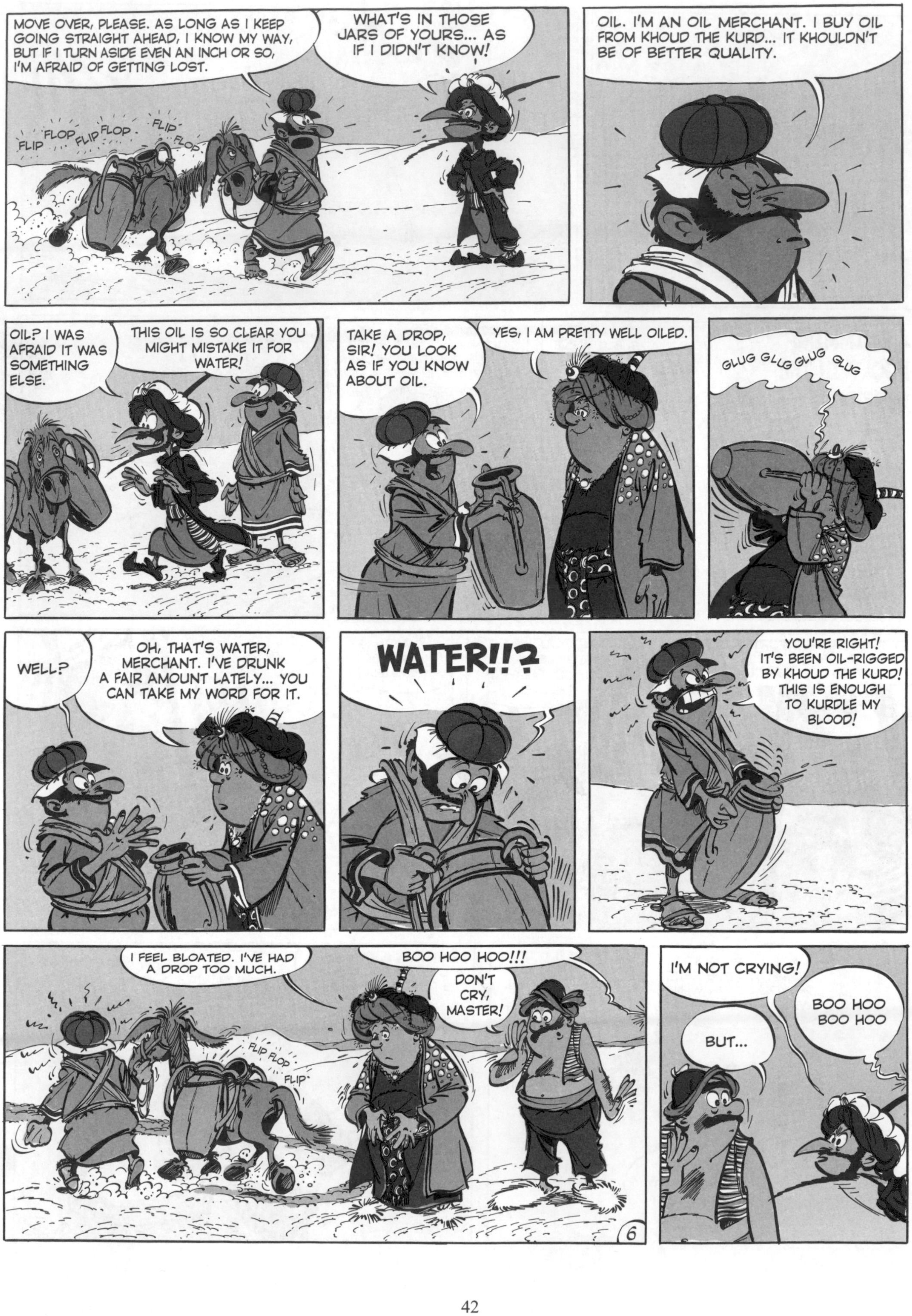
MOVE OVER, PLEASE. AS LONG AS I KEEP GOING STRAIGHT AHEAD, I KNOW MY WAY, BUT IF I TURN ASIDE EVEN AN INCH OR SO, I'M AFRAID OF GETTING LOST.
WHAT'S IN THOSE JARS OF YOURS... AS IF I DIDN'T KNOW!
FLIP FLOP FLIP FLOP FLIP FLOP
OIL. I'M AN OIL MERCHANT. I BUY OIL FROM KHOUD THE KURD... IT KHOULDN'T BE OF BETTER QUALITY.
OIL? I WAS AFRAID IT WAS SOMETHING ELSE.
THIS OIL IS SO CLEAR YOU MIGHT MISTAKE IT FOR WATER!
TAKE A DROP, SIR! YOU LOOK AS IF YOU KNOW ABOUT OIL.
YES, I AM PRETTY WELL OILED.
GLUG GLUG GLUG GLUG
WELL?
OH, THAT'S WATER, MERCHANT. I'VE DRUNK A FAIR AMOUNT LATELY... YOU CAN TAKE MY WORD FOR IT.
WATER!!?
YOU'RE RIGHT! IT'S BEEN OIL-RIGGED BY KHOUD THE KURD! THIS IS ENOUGH TO KURDLE MY BLOOD!
I FEEL BLOATED. I'VE HAD A DROP TOO MUCH.
BOO HOO HOO!!!
DON'T CRY, MASTER!
FLIP FLOP FLIP
6
I'M NOT CRYING!
BOO HOO BOO HOO
BUT...

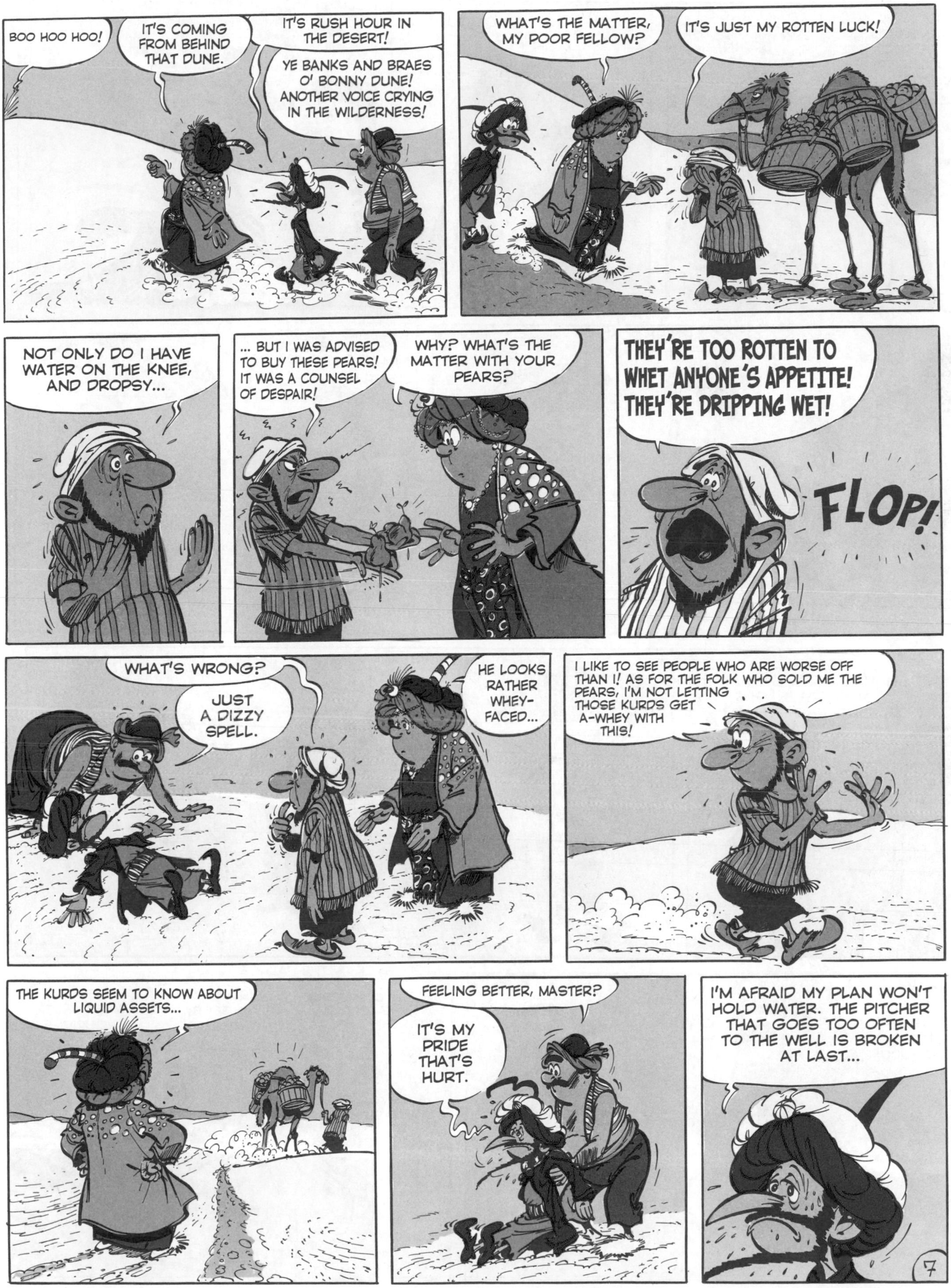

BOO HOO HOO!
IT'S COMING FROM BEHIND THAT DUNE.
IT'S RUSH HOUR IN THE DESERT!
YE BANKS AND BRAES O' BONNY DUNE! ANOTHER VOICE CRYING IN THE WILDERNESS!
WHAT'S THE MATTER, MY POOR FELLOW?
IT'S JUST MY ROTTEN LUCK!
NOT ONLY DO I HAVE WATER ON THE KNEE, AND DROPSY...
... BUT I WAS ADVISED TO BUY THESE PEARS! IT WAS A COUNSEL OF DESPAIR!
WHY? WHAT'S THE MATTER WITH YOUR PEARS?
THEY'RE TOO ROTTEN TO WHET ANYONE'S APPETITE! THEY'RE DRIPPING WET!
FLOP!
WHAT'S WRONG?
JUST A DIZZY SPELL.
HE LOOKS RATHER WHEY-FACED...
I LIKE TO SEE PEOPLE WHO ARE WORSE OFF THAN I! AS FOR THE FOLK WHO SOLD ME THE PEARS, I'M NOT LETTING THOSE KURDS GET A-WHEY WITH THIS!
THE KURDS SEEM TO KNOW ABOUT LIQUID ASSETS...
FEELING BETTER, MASTER?
IT'S MY PRIDE THAT'S HURT.
I'M AFRAID MY PLAN WON'T HOLD WATER. THE PITCHER THAT GOES TOO OFTEN TO THE WELL IS BROKEN AT LAST...
7

AND NOW WE'LL LEAVE YOU HERE AND GO LOOK FOR WATER!

YOU'VE GOT WATER ON THE BRAIN!

OH, LOOK, IZNOGOUD!

GOOD AFTERNOON.

WHAT ARE YOU DOING WITH AN UMBRELLA IN THE MIDDLE OF THE DESERT?

MY DEAR SIR, IT RAINS ONCE EVERY TEN YEARS IN THIS DESERT, AND DO YOU KNOW WHAT DAY IT IS TODAY?

THE TENTH ANNIVERSARY OF THE LAST DAY IT RAINED, TO THE VERY DAY! GOOD AFTERNOON!

I TOLD YOU IT ALWAYS RAINS ON A PICNIC, IZNOGOUD!

AAAAA... CHOOOO!

SCRIPT: GOSCINNY — DRAWING: TABARY -64-

LATER, BACK IN THE PALACE...

WELL, OF COURSE YOU HAVE A NASTY COLD, GETTING DRENCHED THROUGH LIKE THAT!

I'B AFRAID I'VE BET BY WATERLOO!

IT'S ALL WATER UNDER THE BRIDGE NOW...

8

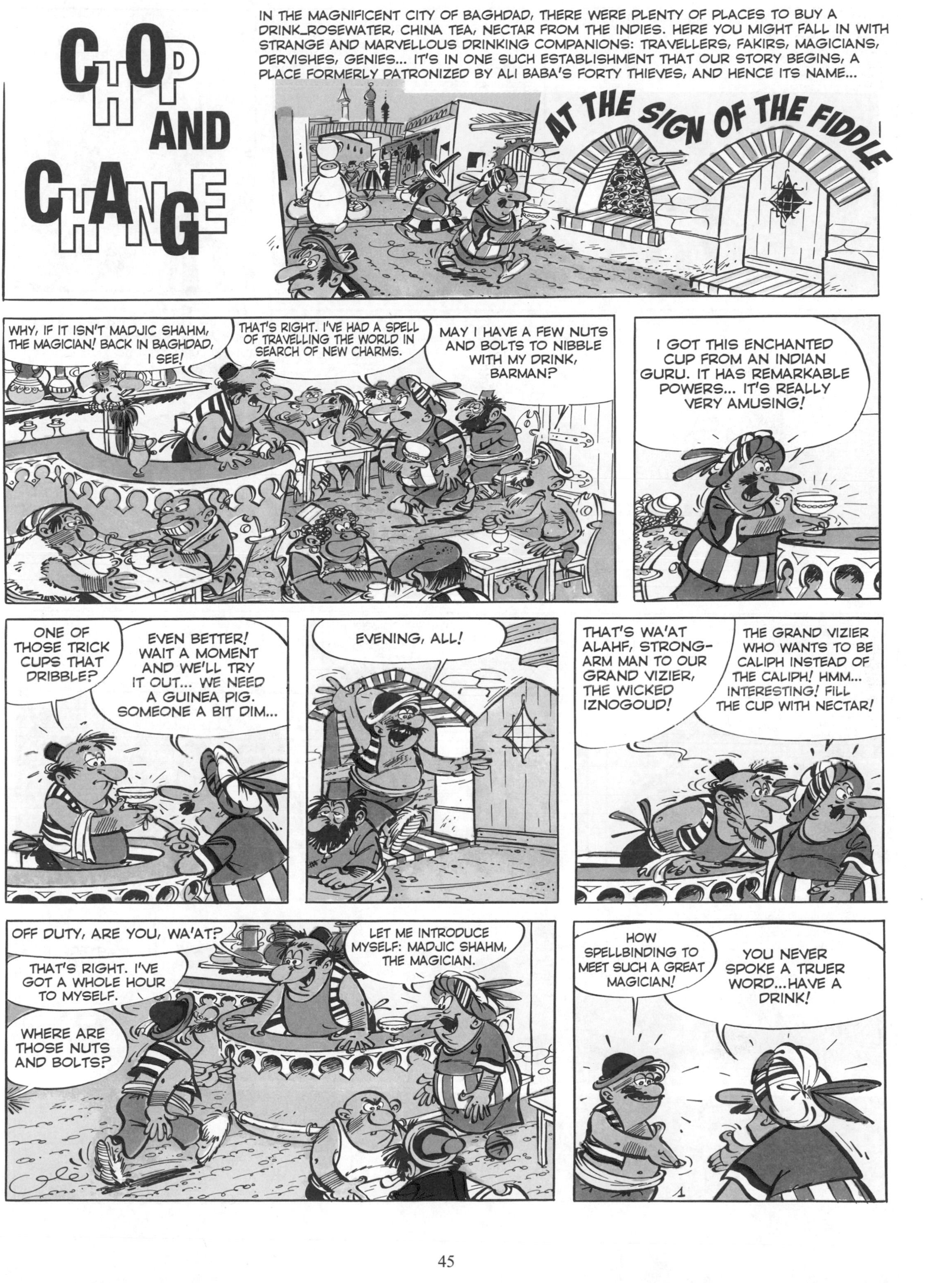
CHOP AND CHANGE
IN THE MAGNIFICENT CITY OF BAGHDAD, THERE WERE PLENTY OF PLACES TO BUY A DRINK_ROSEWATER, CHINA TEA, NECTAR FROM THE INDIES. HERE YOU MIGHT FALL IN WITH STRANGE AND MARVELLOUS DRINKING COMPANIONS: TRAVELLERS, FAKIRS, MAGICIANS, DERVISHES, GENIES... IT'S IN ONE SUCH ESTABLISHMENT THAT OUR STORY BEGINS, A PLACE FORMERLY PATRONIZED BY ALI BABA'S FORTY THIEVES, AND HENCE ITS NAME...
AT THE SIGN OF THE FIDDLE
WHY, IF IT ISN'T MADJIC SHAHM, THE MAGICIAN! BACK IN BAGHDAD, I SEE!
THAT'S RIGHT. I'VE HAD A SPELL OF TRAVELLING THE WORLD IN SEARCH OF NEW CHARMS.
MAY I HAVE A FEW NUTS AND BOLTS TO NIBBLE WITH MY DRINK, BARMAN?
I GOT THIS ENCHANTED CUP FROM AN INDIAN GURU. IT HAS REMARKABLE POWERS... IT'S REALLY VERY AMUSING!
ONE OF THOSE TRICK CUPS THAT DRIBBLE?
EVEN BETTER! WAIT A MOMENT AND WE'LL TRY IT OUT... WE NEED A GUINEA PIG. SOMEONE A BIT DIM...
EVENING, ALL!
THAT'S WA'AT ALAHF, STRONG-ARM MAN TO OUR GRAND VIZIER, THE WICKED IZNOGOUD!
THE GRAND VIZIER WHO WANTS TO BE CALIPH INSTEAD OF THE CALIPH! HMM... INTERESTING! FILL THE CUP WITH NECTAR!
OFF DUTY, ARE YOU, WA'AT?
THAT'S RIGHT. I'VE GOT A WHOLE HOUR TO MYSELF.
WHERE ARE THOSE NUTS AND BOLTS?
LET ME INTRODUCE MYSELF: MADJIC SHAHM, THE MAGICIAN.
HOW SPELLBINDING TO MEET SUCH A GREAT MAGICIAN!
YOU NEVER SPOKE A TRUER WORD...HAVE A DRINK!

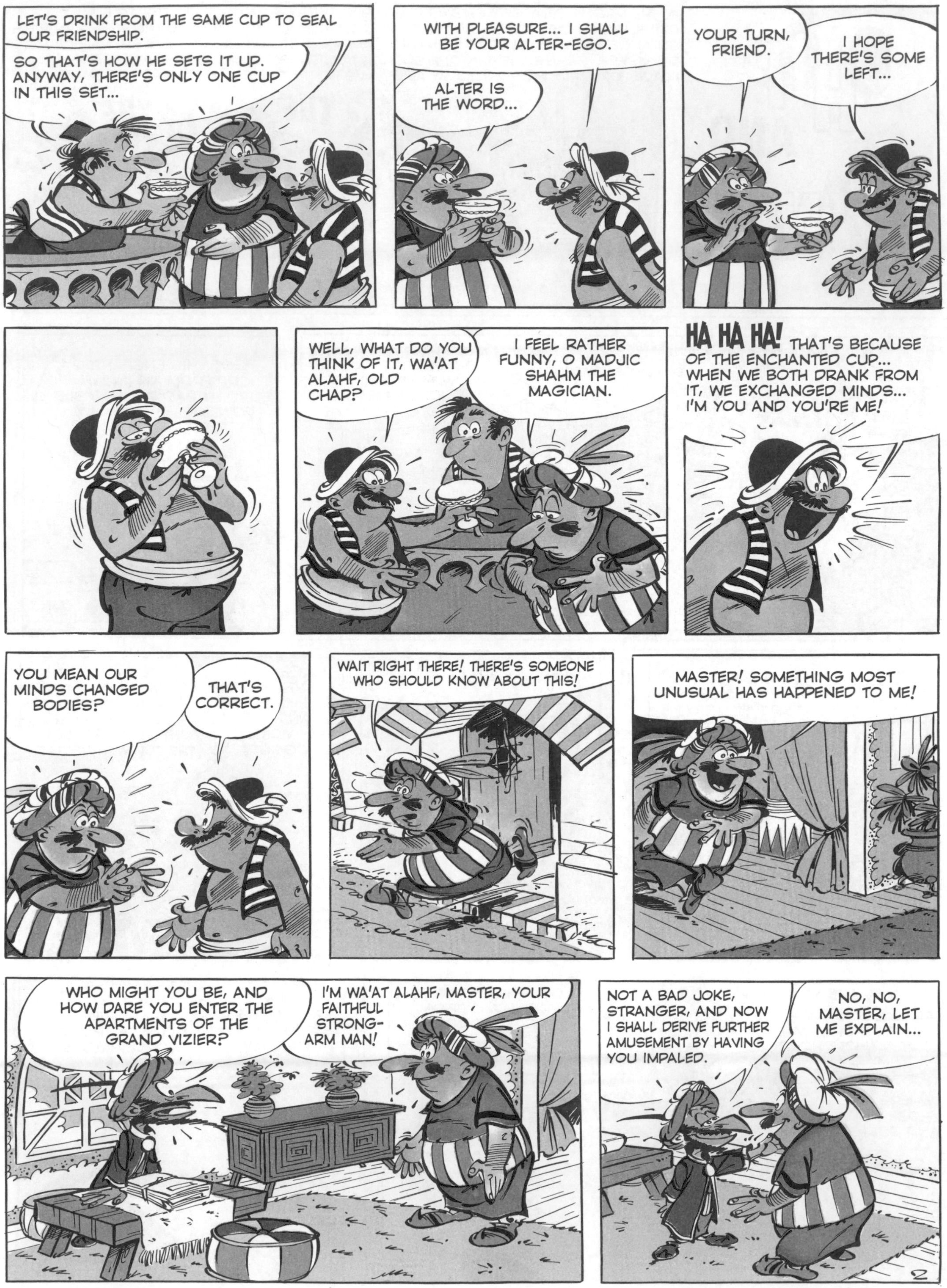
LET'S DRINK FROM THE SAME CUP TO SEAL OUR FRIENDSHIP.
SO THAT'S HOW HE SETS IT UP. ANYWAY, THERE'S ONLY ONE CUP IN THIS SET...
WITH PLEASURE... I SHALL BE YOUR ALTER-EGO.
ALTER IS THE WORD...
YOUR TURN, FRIEND.
I HOPE THERE'S SOME LEFT...
WELL, WHAT DO YOU THINK OF IT, WA'AT ALAHF, OLD CHAP?
I FEEL RATHER FUNNY, O MADJIC SHAHM THE MAGICIAN.
HA HA HA! THAT'S BECAUSE OF THE ENCHANTED CUP... WHEN WE BOTH DRANK FROM IT, WE EXCHANGED MINDS... I'M YOU AND YOU'RE ME!
YOU MEAN OUR MINDS CHANGED BODIES?
THAT'S CORRECT.
WAIT RIGHT THERE! THERE'S SOMEONE WHO SHOULD KNOW ABOUT THIS!
MASTER! SOMETHING MOST UNUSUAL HAS HAPPENED TO ME!
WHO MIGHT YOU BE, AND HOW DARE YOU ENTER THE APARTMENTS OF THE GRAND VIZIER?
I'M WA'AT ALAHF, MASTER, YOUR FAITHFUL STRONG-ARM MAN!
NOT A BAD JOKE, STRANGER, AND NOW I SHALL DERIVE FURTHER AMUSEMENT BY HAVING YOU IMPALED.
NO, NO, MASTER, LET ME EXPLAIN...

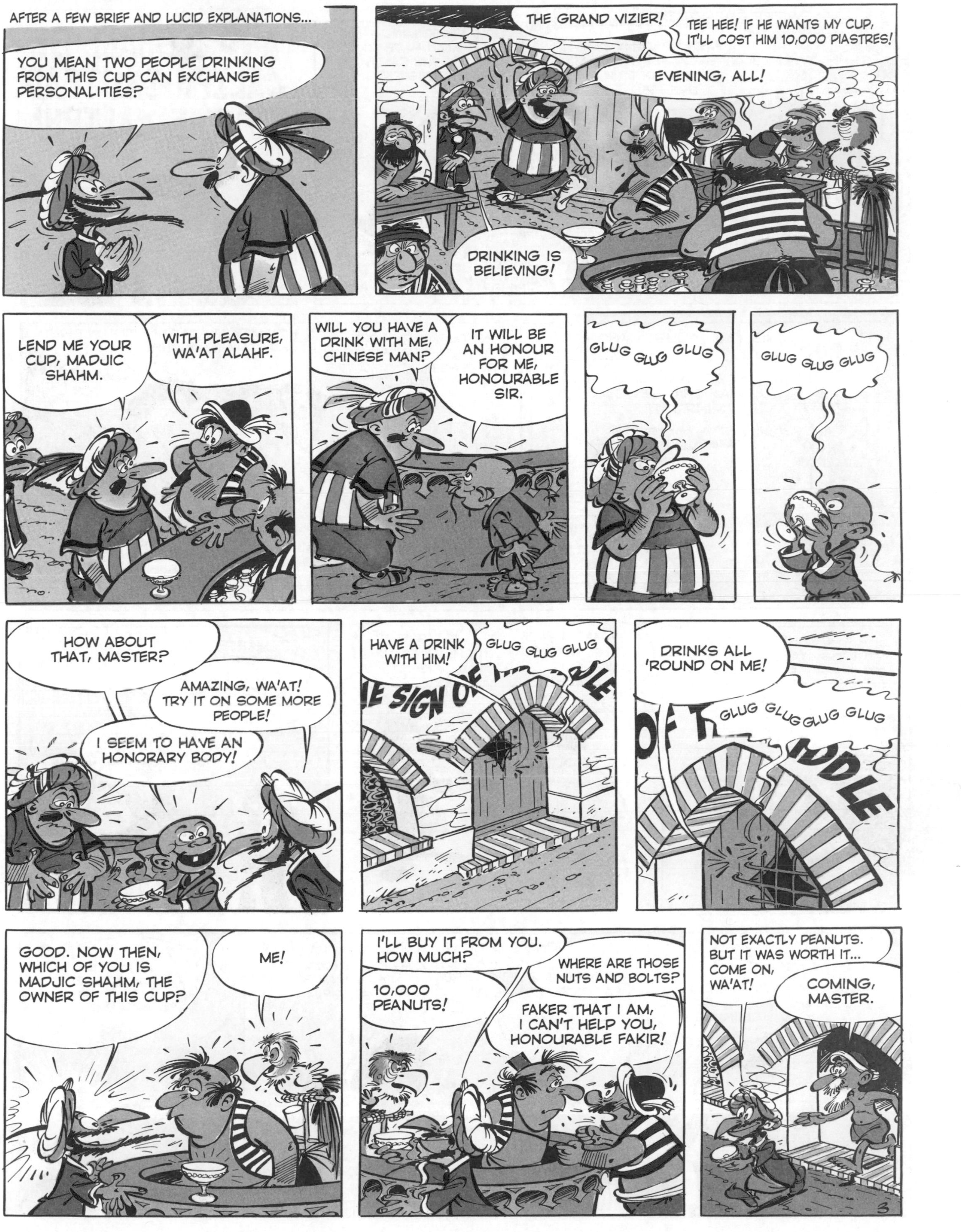
AFTER A FEW BRIEF AND LUCID EXPLANATIONS...
YOU MEAN TWO PEOPLE DRINKING FROM THIS CUP CAN EXCHANGE PERSONALITIES?
THE GRAND VIZIER!
TEE HEE! IF HE WANTS MY CUP, IT'LL COST HIM 10,000 PIASTRES!
EVENING, ALL!
DRINKING IS BELIEVING!
LEND ME YOUR CUP, MADJIC SHAHM.
WITH PLEASURE, WA'AT ALAHF.
WILL YOU HAVE A DRINK WITH ME, CHINESE MAN?
IT WILL BE AN HONOUR FOR ME, HONOURABLE SIR.
GLUG GLUG GLUG
GLUG GLUG GLUG
HOW ABOUT THAT, MASTER?
AMAZING, WA'AT! TRY IT ON SOME MORE PEOPLE!
I SEEM TO HAVE AN HONORARY BODY!
HAVE A DRINK WITH HIM!
GLUG GLUG GLUG
DRINKS ALL 'ROUND ON ME!
GLUG GLUG GLUG GLUG
GOOD. NOW THEN, WHICH OF YOU IS MADJIC SHAHM, THE OWNER OF THIS CUP?
ME!
I'LL BUY IT FROM YOU. HOW MUCH?
10,000 PEANUTS!
WHERE ARE THOSE NUTS AND BOLTS?
FAKER THAT I AM, I CAN'T HELP YOU, HONOURABLE FAKIR!
NOT EXACTLY PEANUTS. BUT IT WAS WORTH IT... COME ON, WA'AT!
COMING, MASTER.

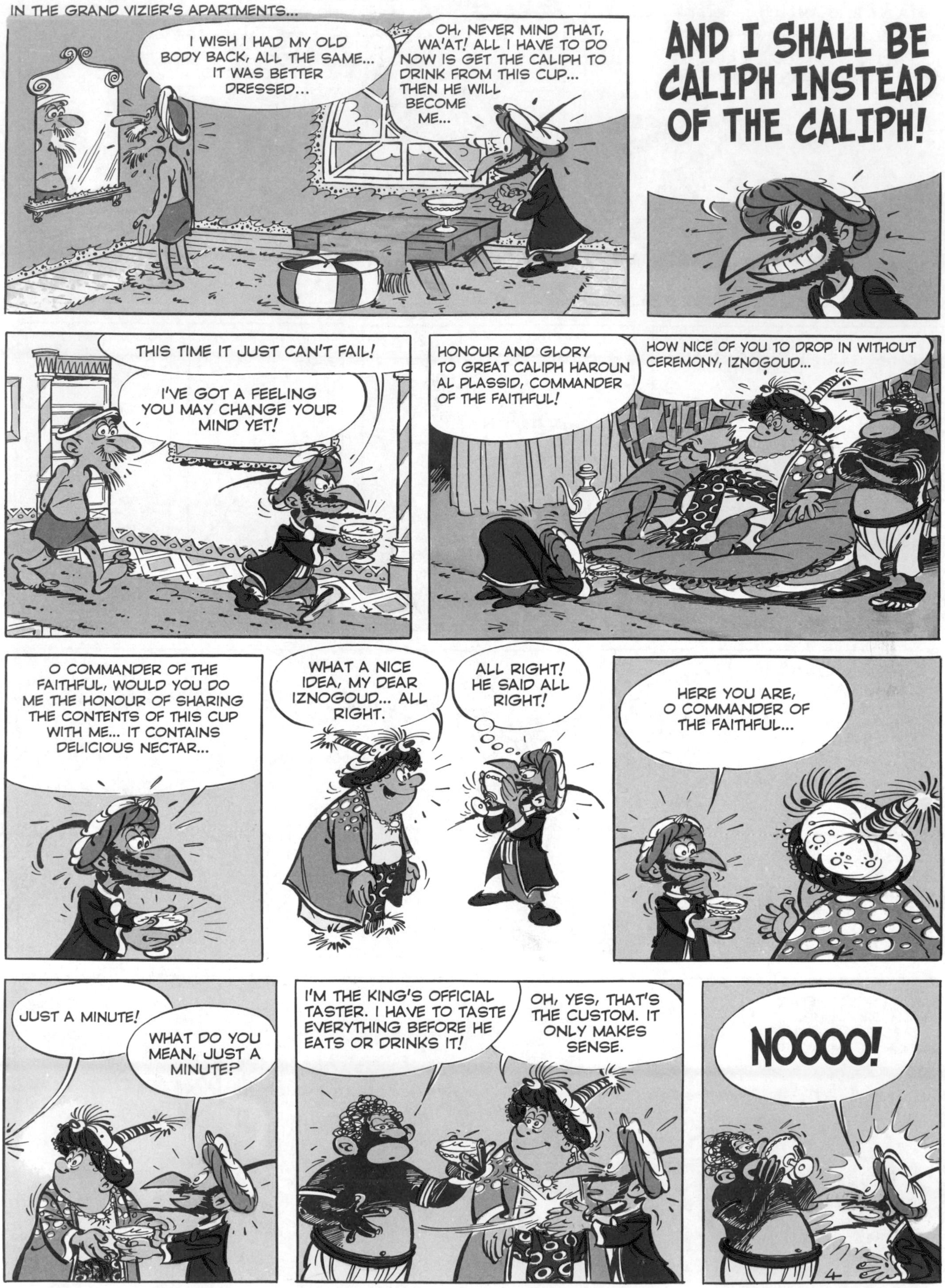
IN THE GRAND VIZIER'S APARTMENTS...
I WISH I HAD MY OLD BODY BACK, ALL THE SAME... IT WAS BETTER DRESSED...
OH, NEVER MIND THAT, WA'AT! ALL I HAVE TO DO NOW IS GET THE CALIPH TO DRINK FROM THIS CUP... THEN HE WILL BECOME ME...
AND I SHALL BE CALIPH INSTEAD OF THE CALIPH!
THIS TIME IT JUST CAN'T FAIL!
I'VE GOT A FEELING YOU MAY CHANGE YOUR MIND YET!
HONOUR AND GLORY TO GREAT CALIPH HAROUN AL PLASSID, COMMANDER OF THE FAITHFUL!
HOW NICE OF YOU TO DROP IN WITHOUT CEREMONY, IZNOGOUD...
O COMMANDER OF THE FAITHFUL, WOULD YOU DO ME THE HONOUR OF SHARING THE CONTENTS OF THIS CUP WITH ME... IT CONTAINS DELICIOUS NECTAR...
WHAT A NICE IDEA, MY DEAR IZNOGOUD... ALL RIGHT.
ALL RIGHT! HE SAID ALL RIGHT!
HERE YOU ARE, O COMMANDER OF THE FAITHFUL...
JUST A MINUTE!
WHAT DO YOU MEAN, JUST A MINUTE?
I'M THE KING'S OFFICIAL TASTER. I HAVE TO TASTE EVERYTHING BEFORE HE EATS OR DRINKS IT!
OH, YES, THAT'S THE CUSTOM. IT ONLY MAKES SENSE.
NOOOO!
4

SURELY I HAVEN'T SUFFERED A CHANGE OF HEART?

WHATEVER IS HAPPENING?

CAN I DRINK THE VIZIER'S HEALTH NOW?

HMM? OH, YES, OF COURSE.

NO, DON'T! THERE'S SOMETHING UNHEALTHY ABOUT THAT DRINK!

BUT YOU OFFERED IT TO ME YOURSELF, MY DEAR IZNOGOUD!

IZNOGOUD? I'M NOT IZNOGOUD! IS EVERYONE CRAZY AROUND HERE?

WAIT A MINUTE. LET ME SORT THIS OUT. THIS IS ALL GETTING A BIT MIND-BOGGLING...

WHO IS THIS?

OH, THAT'S WA'AT ALAHF, MY STRONG-ARM MAN.

LISTEN, MASTER...

NO, I'M YOUR MASTER...

SPEAKING AS AN EXPERT, I'D SAY THIS JOKE IS IN VERY BAD TASTE.

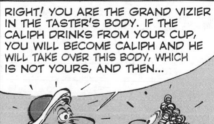

RIGHT! YOU ARE THE GRAND VIZIER IN THE TASTER'S BODY. IF THE CALIPH DRINKS FROM YOUR CUP, YOU WILL BECOME CALIPH AND HE WILL TAKE OVER THIS BODY, WHICH IS NOT YOURS, AND THEN...

HAVEN'T YOU FINISHED YET? I'M GETTING THIRSTY, AND I DON'T UNDERSTAND A WORD OF IT. GIVE ME THAT CUP!

GLUG GLUG

WHY... IT'S WORKING! IT'S WORKING!

Yes, gentle readers, we have been trying to hold you spellbound for a thousand and one nights, and at last it has worked... Iznogoud has taken over the Caliph's body, and thus...

THE CALIPH HAS BECOME CALIPH INSTEAD OF THE CALIPH!

5

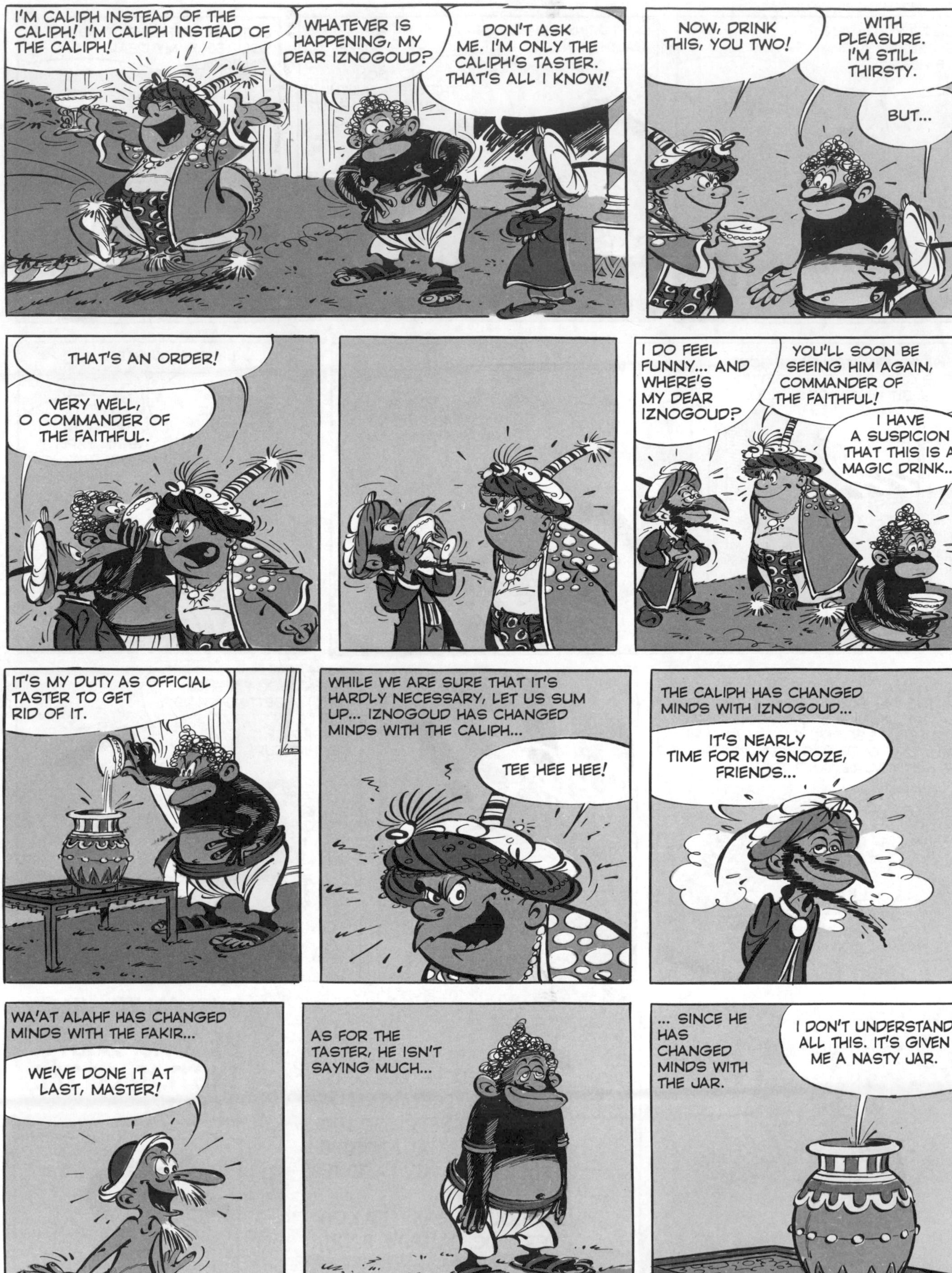
I'M CALIPH INSTEAD OF THE CALIPH! I'M CALIPH INSTEAD OF THE CALIPH!
WHATEVER IS HAPPENING, MY DEAR IZNOGOUD?
DON'T ASK ME. I'M ONLY THE CALIPH'S TASTER. THAT'S ALL I KNOW!
NOW, DRINK THIS, YOU TWO!
WITH PLEASURE. I'M STILL THIRSTY.
BUT...
THAT'S AN ORDER!
VERY WELL, O COMMANDER OF THE FAITHFUL.
I DO FEEL FUNNY... AND WHERE'S MY DEAR IZNOGOUD?
YOU'LL SOON BE SEEING HIM AGAIN, COMMANDER OF THE FAITHFUL!
I HAVE A SUSPICION THAT THIS IS A MAGIC DRINK...
IT'S MY DUTY AS OFFICIAL TASTER TO GET RID OF IT.
WHILE WE ARE SURE THAT IT'S HARDLY NECESSARY, LET US SUM UP... IZNOGOUD HAS CHANGED MINDS WITH THE CALIPH...
TEE HEE HEE!
THE CALIPH HAS CHANGED MINDS WITH IZNOGOUD...
IT'S NEARLY TIME FOR MY SNOOZE, FRIENDS...
WA'AT ALAHF HAS CHANGED MINDS WITH THE FAKIR...
WE'VE DONE IT AT LAST, MASTER!
AS FOR THE TASTER, HE ISN'T SAYING MUCH...
... SINCE HE HAS CHANGED MINDS WITH THE JAR.
I DON'T UNDERSTAND ALL THIS. IT'S GIVEN ME A NASTY JAR.

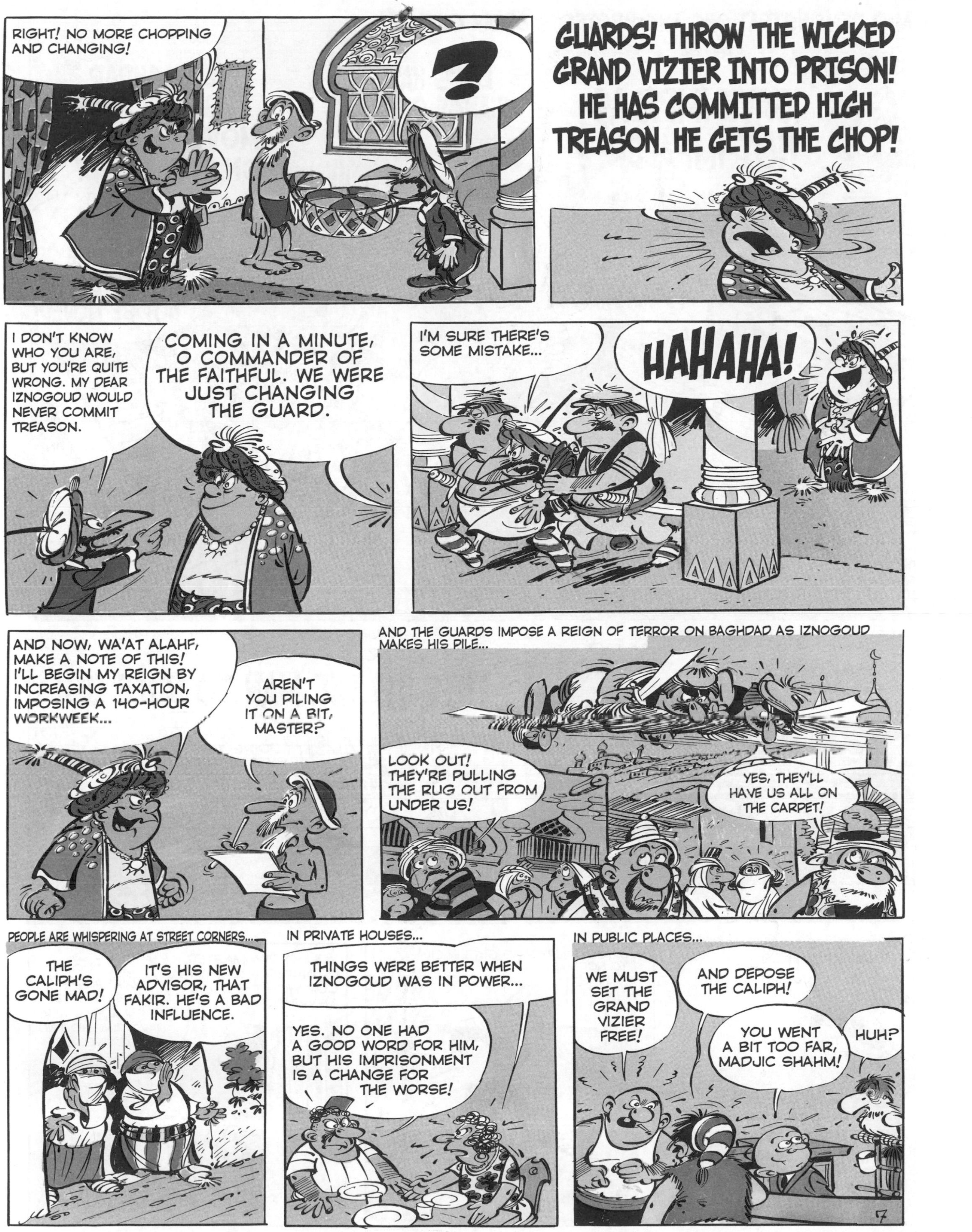
RIGHT! NO MORE CHOPPING AND CHANGING!
?
GUARDS! THROW THE WICKED GRAND VIZIER INTO PRISON! HE HAS COMMITTED HIGH TREASON. HE GETS THE CHOP!
I DON'T KNOW WHO YOU ARE, BUT YOU'RE QUITE WRONG. MY DEAR IZNOGOUD WOULD NEVER COMMIT TREASON.
COMING IN A MINUTE, O COMMANDER OF THE FAITHFUL. WE WERE JUST CHANGING THE GUARD.
I'M SURE THERE'S SOME MISTAKE...
HAHAHA!
AND NOW, WA'AT ALAHF, MAKE A NOTE OF THIS! I'LL BEGIN MY REIGN BY INCREASING TAXATION, IMPOSING A 140-HOUR WORKWEEK...
AREN'T YOU PILING IT ON A BIT, MASTER?
AND THE GUARDS IMPOSE A REIGN OF TERROR ON BAGHDAD AS IZNOGOUD MAKES HIS PILE...
LOOK OUT! THEY'RE PULLING THE RUG OUT FROM UNDER US!
YES, THEY'LL HAVE US ALL ON THE CARPET!
PEOPLE ARE WHISPERING AT STREET CORNERS...
THE CALIPH'S GONE MAD!
IT'S HIS NEW ADVISOR, THAT FAKIR. HE'S A BAD INFLUENCE.
IN PRIVATE HOUSES...
THINGS WERE BETTER WHEN IZNOGOUD WAS IN POWER...
YES. NO ONE HAD A GOOD WORD FOR HIM, BUT HIS IMPRISONMENT IS A CHANGE FOR THE WORSE!
IN PUBLIC PLACES...
WE MUST SET THE GRAND VIZIER FREE!
AND DEPOSE THE CALIPH!
YOU WENT A BIT TOO FAR, MADJIC SHAHM!
HUH?
7

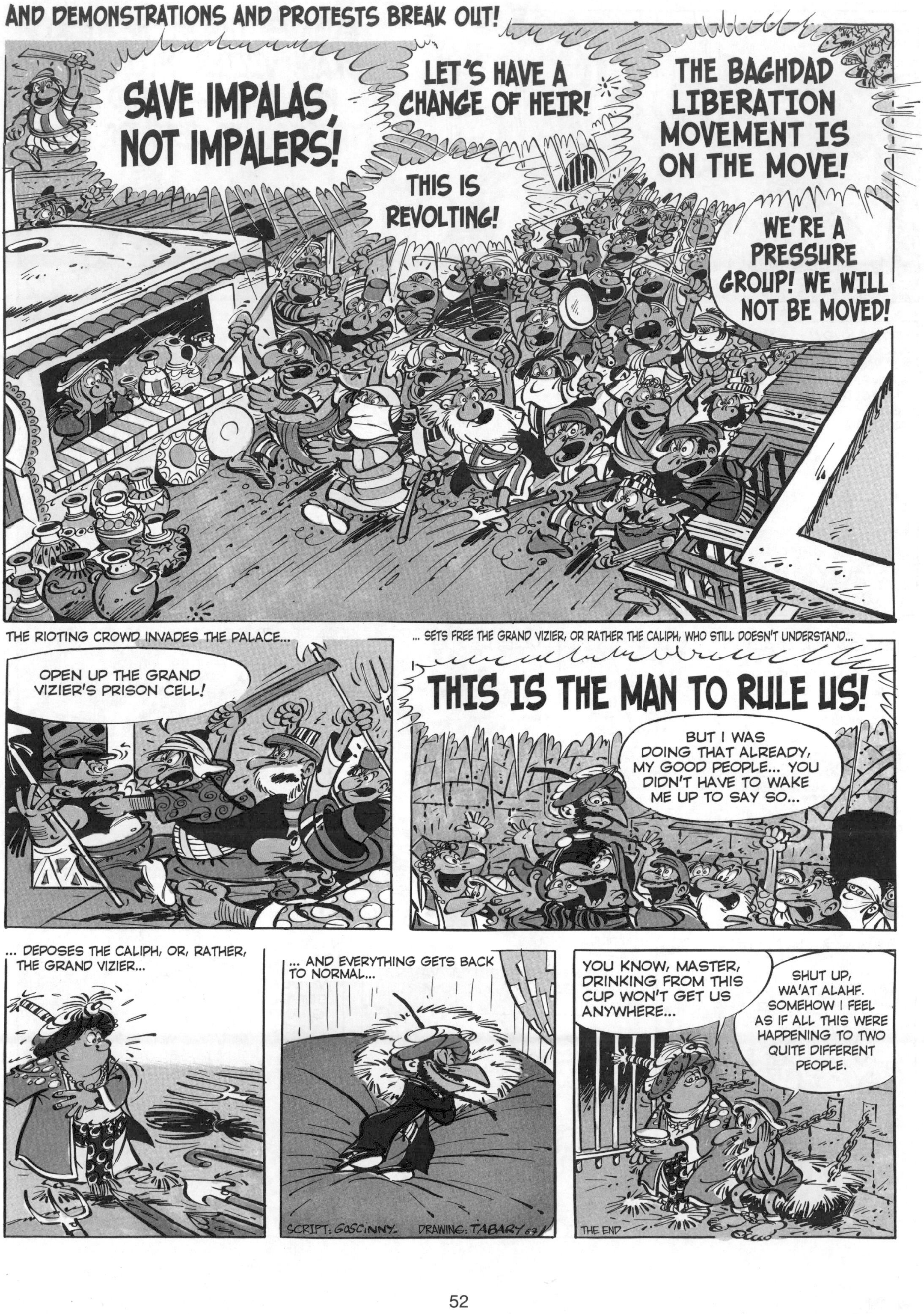
AND DEMONSTRATIONS AND PROTESTS BREAK OUT!
SAVE IMPALAS, NOT IMPALERS!
LET'S HAVE A CHANGE OF HEIR!
THE BAGHDAD LIBERATION MOVEMENT IS ON THE MOVE!
THIS IS REVOLTING!
WE'RE A PRESSURE GROUP! WE WILL NOT BE MOVED!
THE RIOTING CROWD INVADES THE PALACE...
OPEN UP THE GRAND VIZIER'S PRISON CELL!
... SETS FREE THE GRAND VIZIER, OR RATHER THE CALIPH, WHO STILL DOESN'T UNDERSTAND...
THIS IS THE MAN TO RULE US!
BUT I WAS DOING THAT ALREADY, MY GOOD PEOPLE... YOU DIDN'T HAVE TO WAKE ME UP TO SAY SO...
... DEPOSES THE CALIPH, OR, RATHER, THE GRAND VIZIER...
... AND EVERYTHING GETS BACK TO NORMAL...
SCRIPT: GOSCINNY DRAWING: TABARY 67
YOU KNOW, MASTER, DRINKING FROM THIS CUP WON'T GET US ANYWHERE...
SHUT UP, WA'AT ALAHF. SOMEHOW I FEEL AS IF ALL THIS WERE HAPPENING TO TWO QUITE DIFFERENT PEOPLE.
THE END